A Circle of Time

A Novel

Margaret C. Offenberger

Acknowledgements

I wish to acknowledge the generous support of my family and friends. A special thank you to Linda Donahue, Maryann Farina, and Carol Gorman for their comments and support and to Frances Sinon for editing this manuscript.

Dedication

To the people who touch and enrich my life especially Walter, Anne Margaret, Joan, André, Michael, and all the Cahills.

I once suggested to a group of women that it would be fun for
us to write a story or stories about our childhood.
I was told
that that was impossible since everyone had a childhood
that was so normal there was nothing to say.
Everyone
has at least one story.

The Short Necked Puffin

The short-necked Puffin's world
Is etched like crooked lines in sand
Where each cruising, salting, wave,
Which climbs the shore
Or fly by night wind
Cruising through,
Feels free to rearrange
The cosmic scene,
To shift existing symmetry.

There are no steady landscapes.

MCO

If you do not have a story
You do not have a soul.

David McCullough

One

Putty never calls me so when I heard her voice; I knew it was something ominous. I knew the day would come but put off thinking about it for many years. After all, Stokes Pines was part of my past; a part I purposely expelled from my mind for it was a much too painful reminder of my childhood. Although Stokes Pines was the better part, of an untidy childhood it was still painful. Like scraps of paper strewn on a messy desk, it was never quite cleared up but followed me into adulthood.

March was practicing to whistle in with the winds of an angry spring to blow away a winter which left New York City reeling under masses of snow, stained black from the carbon monoxide of a million cars all eager to sit in the same six feet of space. City mass transit is good but as somebody said, "New Yorkers have their cars tied to their asses." It was a long rampageous winter, which conspired to keep people indoors for days on end. Business was at a standstill. The real estate business smoldered to an ember in the wake of a burned out world economy. I was looking to relocate my business to cheaper rent. There were "To Rent" signs popping up all over town. My once greedy landlord anxious to squeeze every penny out of tenants was now willing to the reconsider terms of my lease. However, I determined that a location on Fifth Avenue could now be had for about what I was currently paying to be housed on Second Avenue. Perhaps I could even do better. Second Avenue was littered with antique shops and trendy restaurants that catered to the exotic tastes of the assorted ethnic groups of the city. Our real estate business is located on the third floor over a Thai restaurant. These odors are strange to my meat and potatoes Irish nose. Next door, the odors of gyros dipped in hot grease emanate from the Greek restaurant below. A commercial real estate business can operate out of a less expensive location but Fifth Avenue is prestigious so why not.

Leonard located a space on the second floor in the building contiguous to the one housing Lord & Taylor Department Store and was talking to the landlord. The building, recently renovated, was equipped with the amenities necessary for the high-tech business environment of the day. There was a conference room, five small offices each facing Fifth Avenue, a battery of phone lines and enough outlets to keep an army plugged into the Internet. For me the attraction was the ability to run into Lord & Taylor's between appointments.

Business was bad; we only had one important contract pending. A major corporation was looking to relocate from the mid-west to the lower eastside of Manhattan. Nearly all the "*T-s*" were crossed and all the "*I-s*" dotted so it was a perfect time for me to leave things in Leonard's hands and head south but I was hesitant. In my heart I knew that the excuses I told myself were just that, excuses.

Leonard was my partner, in-house attorney, and recently my lover. We met in college and dated for a time before he met Whitney and got her pregnant. As the noble gentleman he fancied himself, they married and after graduation and law school, set up a home in Westchester along with dozens of their ilk. Their three children, Leonard junior, Abby, and Jodie arrived in quick succession. They settled into a life of Junior League, country club, golf, and martinis - the American dream.

He made partner after three years – right on schedule, however, corporate law, like porcupine needles, dug into Leonard's soul - an irritation but not fatal. That was ten years ago. We ran into each other when my attorney left the firm and Leonard was assigned to take over my account. I was surprised at how he had aged and convinced that time was more sympathetic to me than to him. The beginnings of gray sprouted in the temples of his black hair. The lines around his eyes and mouth were deep set and strained. His eyes, always alive and curious were now dull and staring out at nothing, not interested in anything. There was a sense of living by rote repetition and not by the excitement in the joy of life that I loved in him when we were younger. He was dead on the inside. I wondered what happened to him. However, that was Whitney's problem, not mine.

He negotiated the terms and drew contracts for our real estate transactions. Meetings with clients often went well into the evening hours. It became our custom to grab a bite to eat before he took the train back to Westchester. I should have seen the signs but it all seemed so natural and so comfortable. We were old college friends. I attended their society wedding at the Scarsdale Country Club. True, we lost track of each other after that. He concentrated on paying his dues by putting in the eighteen-hour work- days required of attorneys serious about making partner. I was struggling to build a real estate business.

Leonard saw himself as an insignificant hitchhiker who caught a ride with the big boys of power but was not enjoying the journey. He had no control over his life either at home or at work. It was not long before our dinner conversation turned to strategies for bringing him into the real estate business. I needed help and it would be much less expensive to have a partner who was also an attorney. It was a win win situation.

Whitney did not share this view. For her, the fifty per cent cut in income meant she must curtail her life style. Leonard fruitlessly tried to persuade her, given time, things would improve. He would be happier and so would the family. He needed the control over his life that was not possible in a large law firm but more than possible in a small real estate business. It was no use. However, he was determined and we became partners by the end of the year.

Putty reminded me that we promised to be there for Sara whenever she needed us. That was many years ago but Putty was keeping me to our girlhood pact. Sara was in the Taylorville General hospital as a result, of a massive heart attack. No one knew where her daughter Hilary could be found. Mother and daughter had not spoken in years. It was time to go to Stokes Pines. Leonard did not understand why this was my

5

problem and why the urgency. "What happened, happened years before," he insisted. I had to go, Sara was the woman who saved my life.

Getting to Stokes Pines was more of a task now than it was when I was a child. In those days, it was a two-day car trip. Today, with speed as the god of travel, it behooved you to only visit places with airports. The airline industry had never heard of Stokes Pines. It was barely aware of Fayetteville, North Carolina. I bought a stand-by ticket and was lucky enough to trade it in for a seat on the afternoon plane.

Leonard and I worked out the last minute details of what had to be done in the next few days. I dashed back to my apartment, threw a few things into an overnight case, and headed for LaGuardia. In Fayetteville, it was necessary to rent a car for the two hundred mile drive to Stokes Pines.

Two

As the Continental plane droned on, my mind turned to that fateful evening so many years ago. It was as though it was only yesterday. The mottled sounds of night in that deserted part of town dropped loud and chintzy like a chippy's trinkets on city cement. The lonely buildings of Canal Street stood posturing as some theory of eternity, longing for things that do not change. But that was to be a night of change. There are life-altering decisions, which like a pebble skipped over a pond of water, span out, and ripple in all directions. A life calligraphy completely re-penned in an instant. Tonight was such a night.

We were just back from Florida. My brother Jack had bad lungs and was subject to heavy winter colds and pneumonia. It was decided that the warm climate of Florida would be good for him. She suspected there were other reasons for getting them out of New York City for the winter. Things were not going well. She was married to a man who was reluctant to settle down to a home and a family. He needed his independence. He needed to be unbound and about town. A wife and two young children did not fit his image of himself. It wasn't a matter of not loving his family; it was more a restlessness inherent in his Irish personality. His spirit of poet and lover demanded freedom from the humdrum of family life. There was nothing nine to five in his life at work or at home. She suspected there was someone else. She was desperate.

She said she would be back in ten minutes. The taxi driver waited. The meter was running. Ten dollars and eighty cents was showing. The woman did not look as though she was able to handle that much cab fare. A thin blue cotton print dress, the victim of several dozen launderings, and a dreary mint green short-sleeved sweater were all she wore against the still chilly New York City weather. The two kids asleep in the back seat looked to be about two and six. The cabby wanted to get home. It was a long day. Over the Brooklyn Bridge and on to Bay Ridge, a cold beer and a dinner his wife would reheat. An hour passed. She did not return. Another hour limped by. Eight o'clock at night in the downtown financial section of the city is dark and depressing. The streets are given over to the vermin scrambling to clean up the crumbs left

8

from half-eaten hot dogs and salty pretzels. All human life escaped on the subway hours ago.

The clang of sanitation trucks, scooping the mounds of paper generated during the day, are the only sound to echo through the canyons of tall buildings. It was clear she did not intend to return. The driver woke the girl, the older one. He wanted answers. He needed to get help. What he didn't need were two kids asleep in the back seat of his car. It was usual for passengers to leave things in his taxi. He once found a diamond bracelet worth ten thousand dollars. He even helped deliver a baby. The grateful mother named the baby after him and invited him to the Christening. That was years ago. Tonight he did not need adventure.

Alice left Jack and me in a taxicab about two blocks from Dad's office. She knew I could rattle off the office telephone number. A phone call and the driver was able to deliver us to Dad. This is how Jack and I were separated and thus raised by different people in different parts of the country.

My father was a linotype operator for a printing firm, which specialized in legal printing. The law profession is rarely effected by bumps in the economy. Even in hard times, the courts were grinding away, thus the demand for printed legal briefs and appeals did not wane. Although wages were not high, at least there was steady work. Dad worked nights. He was the only man on the night detail. Working with the hot lead of the linotype machine was sweaty business. There was no air conditioning in those days. As the only person in the shop, he often worked in his underwear. Union rules would not let a linotype operator produce more than ten galleys of type during a shift. While it took most men seven hours to do this, Dad was able to do it in about four. His routine was to begin work at four in the afternoon and finish about eight. After that, it was out with the boys for the evening. This night was different. This night was to change all of our lives.

The all-night diner on Court Street was where I met Sara for the first time. What is it about diners that they become the scene of so many of the important and emotional moments in our lives? When lovers quarrel one or the other will run off to the diner to sit in a dark corner hoping to be joined by the beloved for a tearful and poignant kiss-and-makeup cup of coffee. It is often the low overhead office for the working bookie or numbers runner or the ambulance-chasing attorney. It is the conference room for the small-time dealmaker or the hustler who needs to remain as anonymous as possible. It is the after Church Sunday morning brunch site for the devout. Diners are comfortable like being at home in your kitchen in slippers and bathrobe. It is the social club for the mole people, the all night workers. You can count on the food; standard, deep fried and copious; coffee malodorous as boiling tar.

It was late, about ten o'clock. Jack was asleep with his head on the table. I struggled to stay awake. We never ate in restaurants, so this was a special treat. We sat in a booth in the rear of he diner. The leather bench had a minor tear, which got bigger as each new patron slide over it to scrunch against the wall making room for another person. The odor of days old deep fried onions hung in layers; the faded ivy print wallpaper speckled with years of grease and splattered food particles. The workmen, like old school chums, accustomed to meeting the same persons at the same place, narrated the trivia of their lives between masses of burgers and beer. The waitress, a woman of mid-twenties and questionable blond hair, navigated mountains of food through the narrow aisles separating tables and through the continuous flow of barbs and comments about her beauty and sexiness that churned out from the mouths of her regular customers. She knew them each by name. She knew about their wives and kids. She knew who smoked too much and who drank too much. She knew more about them than their wives. They chided each other as old friends or as kissing

11

cousins might do as this is their home away from home.

Dad needed someone to take care of Jack and me. He was completely unprepared to care for two young children by himself. In his cosmic view, that was women's work. Men were the breadwinners; women remained in the home with complete charge of children. Childcare, home maintenance and attendance to the needs of her husband were the reasons women were created. He was not alone in this view. It was an article of faith for the male of the species of his generation and one institutionalized by the paternalistic hierarchy of the Church.

The early spring New York City evening was chilly. Sara's entrance in her opulent ranch mink coat was a happening to the sanitation workers, policemen, and office cleaning crews who frequented the diner. The titter from the patrons eating at the counter suggested they had decided she was either a high class uptown call girl or she was here to meet her mob lawyer because she had killed her husband to collect the insurance money. They were puzzled about the presence of two small children. In any event, Sara was out of place in this all night diner. To me she was the tallest most glamorous woman I ever met. She was slightly shorter than Dad's six feet. She looked like many of the women I saw in the

12

movie fan magazines. She wore diamond rings on both hands and on four fingers, a necklace of emeralds and diamonds. She spoke softly, slowly, gently, in the manner of a southern gentlewoman. Although half asleep, I was mesmerized, and I was convinced I was meeting a celebrated movie star.

Over second-rate diner pasta, he told Sara that we had been abandoned in a taxicab. His wrath showed in the purple bulge throbbing in his neck as he explained to Sara why he needed her help.

Three

It was late evening when we landed. I picked up a compact car at Avis and headed off toward Stokes Pines, my mind still ruminating on the early days when I first met Sara. I was anxious to see Putty after so many years. As children, we were best friends in the summer and pen pals during the rest of the year. Her mom and dad were tobacco sharecroppers, too poor to own as much as an acre of land in the days when an acre could be purchased for five dollars. She and her brother Jake were the youngest in a family of five children. In our youth, she, Jake, and I were partners in crime. We spent many hours roaming the forests of the Blue Ridge Mountains looking for treasure and for excitement. We never found treasure but were able to spin tall tales around pieces of cast off horseshoes or other debris we found. We once came upon a mound of dirt with an un-inscribed gravestone on it. We were sure it was the body of a fallen Confederate soldier. We secretly tended the gravesite by pulling weeds and planting flowers.

Another day, as we ventured into the back hills, we saw buzzards circling in the sky waiting to descend on their prey. We came upon the half buried decaying body of a horse. Jake recognized it as the horse that once belonged to a local farmer.

A trail of flattened foliage told us the carcass was dragged through the woods, probably by mules and left there to decompose. There were no pet cemeteries. My northern, city sensibilities were shaken.

When we were teen-agers, I tried to get Putty to come north where she would have the opportunity to make a better life for herself. However, her roots were too much entrenched in the claret clay of her birthplace. She married Ethan and had five children of her own and raised tobacco on the hundred acres Ethan inherited from his father.

It was late evening when I drove up the long driveway to Putty and Ethan's ranch house. It is March and the forsythia lining the driveway was showing the first signs of disgust with winter. A white haze, soon to be yellow, played against the red of the landscape. Putty saw the car and ran to meet me. Although we kept in touch through occasional phone calls and a letter or two, it was more than ten years since we saw each other. She looked a little heavier than I remember and her hair, once blond as putty, now was grayer. She still had her effervescent bounce and alert intelligent eyes. I could see she was happy. A trail of children followed her through the door. The three youngest tried to crawl up my legs so I would hold them. The two older ones detached them and held them in their own arms. Putty and I hugged a long hug as old friends who suddenly realized how much they missed each other, how much their lives were different.

Putty showed me through the house she and Ethan built with the help of her three brothers and Ethan's father and brother. She was especially proud of the bathroom for it was the first time in her life that she did not have to go out to the little house with the half moon on it. "I determined to marry a man who could afford a house with indoor plumbing," she explained.

Ethan came in from the fields. He was a quiet man with a strange darkness about him. He carried his Bible in the back pocket of his coveralls, and then laid it down on the dinner table next to his accustomed seat. There was a certain Cotton Mather sternness about him, which I found unnerving. His fingers showed the permanent yellow green stain of the tobacco farmer. He was not at all the kind of man I imagined Putty would love. He did not smile much but when he spoke, his voice was gentle and affectionate. It was clear the children, as well as Putty, adored him.

Before dinner, we prayed and Ethan read a passage from the Bible. Putty's life was not at all like mine and very different from what I expected to find. What happened to the hell-raising girl I knew? After dinner, I helped Putty shuffle the children off to bed. Luckily, at the airport in New York I remembered to buy presents for the children. I brought coloring books, puzzles, and books for each. It galvanized me as their friend forever.

Finally, Putty and I had time to sit down in her kitchen and talk about Sara. Two days ago as she fixed lunch for herself, she suffered a heart attack. Wallace found her on the floor in her kitchen. She was rushed to the Taylorville General Hospital. The prognosis was not good. She was not responding to treatment and seemed to have given up. Putty had been to see her and she asked to see me. We would head out for Taylorsville, a good twenty miles away, right after breakfast. Ethan would take care of the children.

Putty and I talked on for hours remembering the good times and bad times we shared as children. I called Leonard. He was still in the office. The Drama Queen of Scarsdale called the office four times complaining she could not live in such poverty. She was embarrassed to go to the club. She could not bear to have people know there was trouble in the marriage. She knew they were gossiping behind her back. What had she done to deserve this? Her parents too, were mortified. If not for her, stop this idiocy for the sake f the children.

I went to bed but my mind was still churning up old memories of the early days after I first met Sara. Putty insisted on knowing everything about Leonard. She could not believe that I was still not married. As children, we fanaticized her married to a rich tobacco mogul and me married to a millionaire jet setter.

Four

After our meeting in the diner, Jack and I spent the night and the next two weeks in Sara's two-bedroom Washington Heights apartment. Sara was a collector of antiques. To me the apartment was crammed with musty old furniture. I remember wondering why she did not sell some jewelry and buy new furniture. The Queen Anne chair in the living room, close to the front window was my nemesis. Never before had I been on a high floor in a New York City apartment. It was fun to watch people walking below, and it was fun to drop small items like pebbles or jelly beans on unsuspecting pedestrians.

Each time I climbed up and tried to look out the fifth story window of the apartment, I knocked the chair over. It wasn't long before a hind leg came loose and broke off. I tried to put it back in place and pretend I knew nothing about it. There was a three-foot high white Chinese urn with blue figures on it, just inside the door in the foyer. It was explained to me that it was a "ming' something or other and Jack and I should not go near it. As a matter of fact, we were not to touch anything in the apartment, as each item was priceless and irreplaceable. As I bounced around the apartment trying to avoid bumping into things or breaking things I became aware for the first time of the disadvantages of the so called baby fat that made my body too large for acceptance in fashionable society. I was awkward and calamitous. I began to hate my body. Sara said I moved as though I was barefoot in the briar patch.

Mom and Dad had a series of huge rows on the telephone. She wanted to speak to Jack and me but Dad was so incensed at what happened he would not allow it. Jack and I missed her. We cried ourselves to sleep at night. We did not understand what was happening. She wanted us back. She was sorry for what she had done. She wanted Dad to stop seeing Sara. She wanted the family back together. She left us in the taxi to bring him to his senses. She wanted him to realize what his affair was doing to our family. She wanted her family and her life back. She never meant to give us up. Dad said this was the end of the line. He was going to keep us and he wanted a divorce. After much screaming at each other they decided to compromise. They would get a formal separation; Jack would live with her and I would live with Dad. We parted and I did not see Mom or Jack for many years.

Mom was from Boston and since most of her family lived there she and Jack moved closer to her family. She would now have to find a job and she needed someone to care for Jack while she was working. She and Jack moved in with her sister Sue and Sue's family. Mom took a job as a sleep-in night attendant in a nursing home. Jack began a life as a couch kid in Aunt Sue's home. Dad and I remained in New York. My world was shattered. I was losing the two most important people in my life. It seems like a strange compromise. I did not understand until much later why things were decided as they were.

It was early May and the New York schools were still in session. I was sent to PS 132 in Washington Heights and placed in the first grade. Things were different from Florida. Everyone seemed smarter than I was. My math was awful and reading was a chore. I didn't speak to anyone for fear they would laugh at me. I was an outsider. They knew each other all their lives. They started first grade together and by this time of the school year, they were a closed corporation, or so it seemed to me. Young girls, even as young as six, can be brutally cruel and un-accepting of their peers. The colony hovers around the designated queen bee who rules the worker bees. She decides the social hierarchy; who is in and who is out; who is spoken to and who is the outsider. At the age of six, these young despots have learned well how to wield power. The girls reveled in their clicks and were not about to open the door to a little fat kid from Florida.

The boys wanted to roughhouse, make fun of the girls pull hair, and look up their dresses. They enslaved themselves to the dominant male. They discolored the walls of the boy's lavatory with peeing contests. Penis length was power. Bragging rights belonged to the rhinoceros in the group. Someone was always telling them to pull up their zippers and tuck in their shirts.

My teacher, Mrs. Kirchbaum, was most kind and patient. When all our work was finished, on Friday afternoon she read us fascinating stories. It was then I was able to escape into the magical world of fantasy. A.A. Milne's *Winnie the Pooh* and *The House at Pooh Corners* were my favorites. Without friends, I found Pooh Bear, Piglet and Eeyore very good company. They had a sense of humor and managed to get in and out of difficulty with more grace than I was able to assemble.

The rear of Mrs. Kirschbaum's classroom was an enchanted world of games and puzzles. My favorite was the puzzle of the states of the United States. After a bit I was able to recognize the shape of each state and its place on the map. You were permitted into this world if you completed your assigned work before other students. Once your work was deemed completed and correct, you were free to select any of the games or puzzles on the desks at the back of the room and enjoy yourself. The unspoken message to fellow class members was that you were smarter and faster than they were. It was everyone's goal to get to the play area before others. Mrs. Kirschbaum taught us competition and work ethics as well as the regular curriculum.

For many years, it fell to my lot to be the outsider. I suspect it was what led me to develop a sense of humor; able to see the absurdities in life and in much of human behavior. It is a defense mechanism that has helped me through the many more difficult and absurd life situations I have found myself. It was painful at the time but a good life lesson.

The school playground was different from what I was accustomed to in Florida. A ten-foot high chain link fence enclosed a cement area about the size of a football field. There was no playground equipment. The game of choice was tag. The other game of choice was to follow the dominant male or female around the playground to court favor. It was a senseless game of chasing the queen bee or the rhinoceros from one end of the yard to the other for the sole purpose of allowing the leaders to flaunt their popularity. How much of that behavior we learned in childhood carries over to our adult lives?

Everyone sported a bandage to cover a scratched knee scraped on the hard cement during recess or after school play. Pulling off a scab before it was quite ready to be off was a sport that always gathered a crowd. It was a sacrament of bravery to be able to endure the pain of the yank of the last piece of skin and to risk observing the flow of your own blood. There is a cruelty in children in their eagerness to see the other fellow bleed. In groups of their peers, they are not always the sweet darlings to whom we read bedtime stories. Even among the happy memories of childhood, what adult does not have a horror memory of a contemporary who made his life miserable?

In Florida, the playground was grass; there were swings, slides, and monkey bars. Recess was fun. The sun shone most days or at worst, a few watery clouds strayed by to remind us that not everything is perfect. We never missed school because of snow. Everything has its count-counter-point.

There was no lunchroom at PS 132, so you either had to go home for lunch or go to 181*st* Street to the Automat as I did. At the Automat, you put twenty-five cents in a slot, turned a knob, and out came a sandwich. A dime got you a glass of milk. I loved the Automat. I felt very grown up and able to decide what I would eat. I avoided liver, turnips, and most green vegetables. It was years before I learned the technique of pushing food around my plate to shun eating what I did not like.

Sometimes the window would not open after you inserted the coins. A rap on the window, or rather, several raps on the window would get the attention of the attendant on the other side. At lunchtime or dinnertime, they were busier than squirrels at the bird feeder, refilling the slots with food. It was not a good time for small children to be in the way asking for help. Since no one bothered with anyone else in the restaurant, it was a great place to idle between jobs. With a five-cent cup of coffee, the *New York News* and the *Herald Tribune* newspapers, the unemployed locals settled in for the day. They read the papers from cover to cover, bet on horse races, and stared each other down. Although the same people met there every day and followed the same routine,

25

they did not speak to each other. New Yorkers are private people. Perhaps this is why we have the reputation of being unfriendly.

I was never frightened being in the Automat as a young child alone. Sometimes I had a problem turning a knob or retrieving a sandwich from the slot. Someone was always there to help so I did not have to bother the busy attendants. When the Automat was crowded, two or three strangers shared a table. You found a chair, sat down, and ate. Because I was a child, people often tried to engage me in conversation. I answered questions by saying my mother was shopping next door and would join me in a minute or two. Dad warned me about talking to strangers.

After Jack and Mom left Dad, and I moved in with Sara and Hilary. I missed Jack and Mom and was not pleased with Sara or her daughter. Hilary was about my age. I had to sleep in the same bed with Hilary while Dad and Sara were in another bedroom. I took an instant dislike to her. She was skinny, whiny, and sickly. I was a porker who delighted in eating everything in sight. She had to be coaxed to eat; I had to be coaxed not to eat. She was all party dress; I was all fatty fashion. She always had a runny nose or an upset stomach. I had an iron stomach and an impeccable nose. She was out of school at least one day a week. I was a candidate for the perfect attendance certificate. She was spoiled and I was not. Well, I did not think I was but perhaps there were other opinions on that subject. We spent many of our early days tormenting each other. She cried and ran to her mother to complain about me. I called her a snitch who could not fight her own battles. I was punished a lot. Dad said the only way to keep the peace was for me to be nice to her. It was discriminatory. Why was everything my fault? In all fairness, she was not happy with me either. In those days, oil and water had a better chance of co-existing.

Her father was dead. He died a hero's death in a New York to Bermuda Yacht Race. Benedict Raddy was well known in New York and international boating circles. He loved the sea and the challenge of the race. They were off the south New Jersey coast. No moon; no stars. The only light was the flicker of lanterns from nearby ships. The high winds brought swell upon swell of ocean water crashing over the deck and whipping overboard anything not secured to the deck. Waves, Himalayan height, thrashed crewmembers against the mast. They struggled to right the ship now on the port side; then on the starboard side in an effort to protect from capsizing. Benedict remained at the wheel with the first mate. It took a major effort by the two of them to tack against the wind. A kerosene lantern

27

turned over in the galley and the boat caught fire. In a rolling sea, it was impossible to get below and more impossible to extinguish a fire. The nearby yacht, Sea Challenger, soon observed their distress and came by to help rescue the crew. After several attempts and a brief and welcome calm in the sea, a cable with a pulley from the Sea Challenger was attached to the burning boat. One by one, the crew hung on to the hook on the pulley and transferred to safety. Benedict held the wheel until the others were safely on the other boat. When it was Benedict's turn to be rescued, he deserted the wheel; the boats separated. He was thrown overboard into the raging ocean, dragged under as the boat broke apart from the punishment of the water and the destruction of the fire. His body was never recovered. *The New York Times* headline read, "Millionaire Yachtsman Hero at Sea."

The legend of the exploits of Benedict Raddy, apocryphal and real, was kept alive through bedtime stories, scrapbooks, and newspaper clippings. There were small altars of pictures illuminated with burning candles in each room of the apartment. There were rumors that one of Benedict's grandfathers or great grandfathers served with the United States Army in the Civil War. Colonel Raddy commanded the fifty-third Regiment of New York Volunteers at the Battle of Gross

28

Keys, in the Shenandoah Valley in 1862. However, Colonel Raddy was on the wrong side of the conflict, so his heroic deeds were not spoken aloud but whispered quietly and with expressions of doubt as to their authenticity. The Union Army did not fare well in the battle. A better-positioned Confederate Army drove them off. Bragging rights were a mixed blessing. To celebrate the Confederate victory would suggest Grandpa was a loser. Yet, Sara was secretly proud to think that Grandpa Raddy may have been a proud southern gentleman and soldier defending the glorious south of her birth.

Benedict was a fabric designer who designed the Pullman car for railroads or he designed the fabrics used in the railroad Pullman cars. My lack of clarity on this topic is an indication of my interest in the life and times of the millionaire yachtsman. Nevertheless, I suspect I knew more about her father than I did about mine. Perhaps I was bitchy but I had my own problems. I missed my mother and brother. In addition, my father wasn't around very much. I needed my own heroes, not someone else's. I wanted to go home.

Although there was little talk about it, I realized when I got older that Sara and her husband were divorced before his yacht met its unfortunate end. Sara wanted to preserve the myth that Mommy, Daddy, and Hilary were living happily ever after but in fact, there was a messy divorce. His family wanted no part of Sara or her daughter. As far as they were concerned, Sara was an opportunist hillbilly and a bit of a fallen woman who was not acceptable in their society. Not only that but she was an unemployed actress. The family had other plans for his marriage and career. Benedict had set up a trust fund for Hilary but cut Sara off completely. Each year Sara had to convince the trustees to give her enough money to keep Hilary in the style her husband would want for his daughter. They both lived on the money from the trust and whatever Sara could hustle one way or another. Acting was not paying the bills and an encounter with the good life convinced her she never wanted a real job.

Although uneducated, Sara had an instinctive sense of business. She knew how to use her female attributes to structure a business deal to the envy of many a man. At heart, she was a horse trader and gambler able to parlay her meager financial assets into a relative fortune. Before she was twenty-one years old, she married a wealthy man, adorned herself in diamonds and sapphires, and wrapped herself in mink. For getting along in the world, she was more like her father, Tom Devaux, than any of her siblings.

Her father, Tom, began his career as a tobacco-farming sharecropper and ended as a successful landowner, tobacco farmer, and tobacco manufacturer. He produced twist and plug tobacco; he sold it from the back of his horse-drawn wagon as he traveled the back roads of the Blue Ridge Mountains. The dirt roads were treacherous especially in autumn. Rain-eroded roads left deep crevices and exposed large rocks hazardous to both horse and wagon. He often came home with a different horse due to the need to shoot a horse with a broken leg. There were stories that he had two other families and five other children that he visited on his rounds. Every once in awhile someone turned up in Stokes Pines with the name Deveaux and a father named Tom. Occasionally Sara's mother took into the family a new lad or lass claiming to be a half brother or sister. It depended on how much she needed help on the farm and how good a worker he proved to be. Times were hard; people were poor. A good farm hand was an asset to a labor-intensive tobacco farm no matter whose child he was. The situation of men with multiple families was considered normal especially for men who spent months on the road traveling from place to place. After all, men will be men and women who have no other means of support will let them.

Sara was a Tar Heel out of a small hamlet in the Blue Ridge Mountains of northwestern North Carolina. She was the oldest of eight children. Her French ancestors found their way into the mountains sometime during the seventeen hundreds. They followed the Appalachian Trail down from Pennsylvania; they settled in, married, raised children and tobacco, and never came down the mountain. Many were Moravians looking to find more space to practice their religion and more land to farm. Pennsylvania was getting too overpopulated for these quiet simple life people. Electricity and paved roads did not come to this area until the early nineteen-fifties. Somehow, the Draft Board found them and recruited some to serve in World War II. There was no industry other than tobacco farming.

The thought of marrying a farmer, raising a herd of children, and going through life with hands stained yellowed from tobacco gum, did not appeal to Sara. She left home at fifteen and came to New York. There she hoped to become a film star. She appeared in one or two short silent films but ended her career with marriage to Benedict Raddy, Hilary's father. Benedict, a wealthy New York tycoon, was enchanted with her beauty and her droll Southern accent. An exemplary stage door Johnny, he enjoyed the allure of Broadway and the emerging New York film industry. They were married in an intimate ceremony in the Little Church Around the Corner in Manhattan and rented a penthouse on Park Avenue. Hilary was born six months later.

Sara's next goal was to get her siblings down from the mountain and into New York. She brought her two sisters, Lily and Dorothy, to town, connected them, through friends of Benedict, to the New York scene and married to flourishing businessmen. Lily's marriage to an insurance executive was carried in *The New York Times*. Dorothy married an engineer. They later moved to Virginia and took up residence at the University of Virginia where Couburn taught mathematics. He produced several inventions, which the Department of Defense purchased and integrated into weapons used in the Second World War. Both sisters and their husbands, as was the custom of the day, honeymooned for a month in Europe. They sailed to South Hampton, England, then on to the major cities of the continent.

Sara was not so effective with her five brothers. Each in turn came to New York, stayed a year or two, each returned to North Carolina, and established dynasties in the mountains siring eighteen children among them. Of all the brothers, Harry was my favorite. He was a man of magic and charisma who treated me like a princess. I sat for endless hours listening to the tales of his wild adventures. Everyone needs an Uncle Harry to tell him or her outrageous tales about the wonders of the world. He had been everywhere. He knew all the important people in the South as well as the beautiful people I watched in the movies on Saturday afternoon. In truth, Harry had never been to the exotic places he claimed. He had been to New York once or twice because Sara insisted he try his hand at making a living. He was not good at that. He never had money but he was a rich man who enjoyed everything in life. Some would say he never lived up to his potential. Harry was a happy person.

Even at an early age, I suspected his stories were more fiction than fact but he was fun. He was a dreamer of dreams who had looked at New York City and decided it was not for him. At best, he ventured a few hundred miles around western North Carolina always coming back to his roots. He weaved yarns of mirth and marigolds and children dancing through water sprinklers under the summer sun, and of maharajas of India who lived in golden castles. He allowed me to dream dreams of other lands and other lives. A childhood without a weave of dreams and a weave of the surreal is certainly a deprived childhood. I am grateful for Harry.

Since I was his best audience, he paid much attention to me. He was a tinker of motors. He bought broken down old cars, tinkered with them, drove them around the mountains, and then sold them for more money than they were worth. Treasured memories of my childhood are the days Harry let me ride on the back of his motorcycle. I held on tight to his waist and with hair and clothing blowing in the wind, sped over back roads. My greatest thrill came when I was twelve and he sat behind me as I drove the motorcycle at breakneck speed through the country roads behind Sara's farm. It was the first realization I had of the freedom that comes with *wheels*. From that day forward I dreamed of the day I was to turn sixteen. First I would get a driver's license then a convertible car; a few friends then off to exploration of the world; off to freedom from school, parents, and childhood. How to pay for this never entered my mind. Like Dorothy, Tin Man, and Lion, I was off to find the wizard.

My father was not pleased with my exploits with Harry. I was breaking the law since I was too young to drive and I did not have a license to say nothing of the danger of motorcycles. Harry should know better. Dad and Harry had words about endangering the life of a child. After that, Harry and I did not mention our motorbike trips to anyone. Sara had a different view. She scolded Harry for his recklessness but secretly enjoyed his sense of adventure and my willingness to go along with it. All she said to me was, "Be careful." Harry was my hero!

Harry was a born salesman who could sell the proverbial ice to the icebound. At one point, he actually sold his wife and two children on the benefits of moving in with his mistress and his other two children. Money was tight. If two could live as cheaply as one, surely seven could live on a pittance. **That's** a salesman!

They lived in a rented three-bedroom apartment in Thanville, Virginia a small cotton mill town close to the North Carolina border. Number one wife, Lena worked at the town hospital as a nurse's aide. She was the main support of the family. Number two wife, Hortense, did not work. Raised as a Southern Belle in a family with numerous servants, she did not know how to work. Her wealthy family disowned her when she became involved with Harry, a married, unemployed man. The family owned the Pepsi Cola bottling plant in town and was socially prominent in this small circle of this small town. Their embarrassment was total when Hortense and her two children moved in with Harry's other family. Her life style was an abomination to them. The shock to the sensibilities of small town wags was devastating.

Lena did most of the work both in the house and out. She did the cooking as well. Hortense, accustomed to life among the wealthy, was rather useless when it came to everyday living. Her day consisted of up at the crack of ten, coffee and cigarettes until noon then shower and dressed. Lena appreciated going to her job each morning. It got her out of the house early and away from what might have been full days of tension between the two women. All of the children were of school age so Harry and Hortense were the only after school babysitters until Lena arrived home from work. The children and their mother's came separately to Stokes Pines to visit Sara. Sometimes each family stayed a week or two. When the climate at home in this mingled family got too tense, Harry brought to Stokes Pines the family in most need of a vacation. The children were younger than Hilary and I so we played with them as though they were our live dolls. We dressed them up in our clothes and took them shopping at the general store down the road. We begged money to buy them candy and of course, we had to be treated too. Sara made clothes for all of them. She could not bear to see them in the same dress everyday. Sewing was Sara's passion. She sat at the Singer for hours pumping the pedal, and singing and humming mountain music. It was her way to deal

37

with the absurdity in the lives of the people around her.

Harry supported his unusual family by plying his sales talents to earn just enough money to keep the landlord at bay and just enough food on the table not to listen to the growls of hungry stomachs. Beyond that, he was a man of leisure. His evenings were spent enjoying the company of good moonshine and beautiful women. But you had to love him and scores of women did.

Royce, the youngest, was my other favorite of Sara's brothers. He played the banjo and the guitar day and night. He dreamed of one day going to Nashville to become a famous country singer. However, the time was never right or the bus fare was never there. He talked about Nashville to everyone who would listen. He knew the names of every country singer. His bedroom walls were plastered with their pictures. His special banjo piece was *There's A New Moon over My Shoulder and an Old Love Still in My Heart.* He played it repeatedly. He constantly suffered the loss of a girlfriend who moved on to more marriageable suitors. He never married, and I do not remember him having a job. In summer, he did not move off the front porch. Strumming his banjo was his life. Once in awhile he would make up a song about me and sing it to me if I agreed to fetch him a cold beer. I was in love with him, his handsome face, his pumped iron physique, and his Nashville music.

None of the brothers worked very much. They lived from hand to mouth and, when the distance from the hand to the mouth became too great, they worked just enough to shorten the distance. Sara was the mother hen who berated this lack of industry in her talented but lazy brothers. They each had the business acumen and the charm of their father, but only she had the ambition to do anything with it. I wonder now how Sara tolerated this string of idle family members who imposed on her time and hospitality for so many years. There are seemingly no limits to southern hospitality.

Although Sara became a New Yorker, she never got the red clay of the Blue Ridge Mountains out of her system. She spent summers in the mountains and winters in New York City. After Benedict died, she returned to Stokes Pines, bought a fifteen-acre farm, and built a manor house and small bungalow. The farm and bungalow she rented out to tenant farmers who worked the tobacco crop. She bought the seed, they did the work, and both split the profit. A good year netted enough money to pay her expenses for the farm and her expense to live in Manhattan without dipping into the principal of Hilary's trust fund.

The Manhattan temperatures of ninety-eight and one hundred degrees during July and August felt hotter than the hot chili at the Automat. It burned you from the inside out. The humidity can reach eighty or ninety percent. Sane people abandon this inferno for the mountains or seashore. I was a city kid with little more than ten cents to ride the subway to Coney Island. Sara took me to the farm for the summer. Around the middle of June, she would buy an old model used car. In those days, you could buy an old Ford for about one hundred dollars. It was always black for as Henry Ford said, "You can have a Ford in any color as long as it is black." It had a clutch and a brake and needed endless gear shifting. In the hot weather, the radiator overheated and blew up on a regular basis. Often when we stopped for gas, it was also necessary to patch a hole in the radiator or to replace a radiator. Our long distance driving was an escapade in sputter and spew. These wrecks were so un-road-worthy that we barely made it into New Jersey before it was necessary to stop for repairs. Thanks again, to Henry Ford's concept of interchangeable parts, and the simplicity of the old cars, the mechanic was frequently able to pop in the new part and send us on our way within an hour or so.

By the first of July, after school closed, she, Hilary, and I started out for North Carolina.

Dad had to work so he rarely came along. Things were much better for me when he was around. Hilary was afraid of him, a fear I learned to use to my benefit. In his presence, she was less whinny and more agreeable to me. With dad there, it was my turf. Otherwise, we were on her playing ground and she owned all the marbles.

The journey was five hundred miles and took two days - sometimes three. The Ford or *Flivver,* as we called it, was incapable of a speed of more than fifty miles an hour. Sara was an especially cautious driver probably because she was severely hearing handicapped. I am not sure if the lack of speed was the result of an antique car or Sara's fear of other drivers. She required someone in the front seat to keep her in touch with the sounds of traffic around her. She refused to wear glasses lest she appear less attractive. As she drove, she grasped the wheel with both hands, leaned forward, and squinted to see the road. She was as relaxed behind the wheel as a goya comic headlining in the Borscht Belt.

One year, we drove south in a Ford with a rumble seat. My teeth rattled loose, and the wind and sun augmented my already dappled face with a million more freckles. I got my first sunburn of the season. It was the most fun I had all that year. I remember being so happy to have a car ride, especially in the rumble seat, that it never occurred to me to ask, "Are we there yet?" We never had a car because Dad, as many New York men, never learned to drive. The infrastructure of buses and subways in the city made the expense of owning a car unnecessary. Besides, prices would come down. According to my father, prices were always too high and would of necessity, come down. It was a flaw in his character; he always thought he was being cheated. Perhaps it was the New Yorker in him to be suspicious of everyone. He bought nothing unless he knew a "guy in the business" who would give him a "good deal"

There were no super highways. We passed through the major cities going south - Philadelphia, Baltimore, Washington, Richmond. We usually stayed over night in Richmond at the home of a relative. As you may have heard, all Southerners are related. There is a joke that circulates in the north. It asks the question, "If two Southerners get divorced are they still cousins?" First cousin, Uncle Joe Bob, was a hunting and fishing man as well as a tobacco farmer who lived with his wife and four boys on one hundred fifty acres just north of Richmond Virginia. They raised hound dogs for hunting opossum. When we got out of the car dogs swarmed over us leaving muddy paw prints on crisp clean cotton dresses. Tails wagging they howled and yelped in a frenzy of friendliness, happy to see new faces.

We were always greeted with quantities of southern fried chicken, hot biscuits, and corn bread. No southern meal is complete without biscuits and corn bread. Within minutes after our arrival, Uncle Joe Bob's wife stood at the open kitchen window with her twenty-two gauge rife and shot a Rhode Island red rooster through the head. She announced, "Dinner will be ready in an hour, ya'll."

The sons were not friendly. They were at an age where they did not like girls. They wanted to wrestle while we preferred dolls. It was not a good match up. I was happy to see morning and get back on the road. They packed a lunch for us of chicken and corn bread. Sara, cousin Bob, and his wife stayed up late to talk and to drink. As a result, it was past noon when we were able to pack ourselves back into the car and be on our way.

After Richmond, it was into the Blue Ridge Mountains and miles of dirt roads. After a rainstorm, and it always seemed to be raining, we sloshed along in slippery red mud that reached up to the running board. When you got out of the car, you removed your shoes and carried them to a dry spot before putting them on again. Slimy red mud between your toes is a delightful, sensual, fleshy, almost sexual treat but red mud-drenched wet clothing is as erotic as sawdust.

Sara believed that city kids should learn something about rural life. Summer on the farm was a time to experience how the other-half lives. This summer on the trek to Stokes Pines, she stopped at a chicken hatchery. They loaded five hundred fuzzy round yellow baby chicks into the car. They were the size of the peepers I remember seeing in New York around Easter time. They squealed and pecked each other as they fought for space and position in the confined area of the crate in which they were packed. *Pecking order* had new meaning for me! It led me to thinking about other expression I heard and to wondering about where they originated. What does *red-up* mean for instance and where did it come from? Everyone south of the Mason-Dixon line says it. I determined to pay more attention to these expressions and see if I can figure them out. In any event, we lost five chicks before we got to Stokes Pines. Their siblings managed to crush them in the confined quarters of the crate. I wanted to give them a proper burial by the side of the road but Sara dismissed this idea saying we had no time for this silly city girl foolishness. It took me nearly a day dealing with liquid eyes before I got over it. I wanted to take the chicks out and play with them but Sara warned they were not pets they were products. If we were to become attached to them, how would we be able to take them to market? I wasn't sure I wanted to take them to market. The thought of them becoming Sunday dinner was stomach turning. Little did I know that the day was coming when that would sound like a capital idea.

The project for this summer was to tend these chicks until they were *fryer* size and sell them to the locals. Southern fried chicken is legendary. We were to be in on the beginning. It was a lesson in taking responsibility and in good business practice. If nothing else, Sara was a good businesswoman. It was also meant to educate the city kids that food doesn't just come from the supermarket.

The chicks were to be the sole responsibility of Hilary and me. Sara set them up in the hen house out near the tobacco barn on her farm. She bought feed, gave us a bucket, and showed us where to get water for our wards. She provided a shovel for cleanup duty and promptly abandoned the project.

Three-day or four-day old chicks are cute one at a time at Easter along with the chocolate the Easter Bunny brings. However, five hundred at a time are work. There was no electricity on the farm. Therefore, there was no running water. Every drop of water those chicks drank was drawn from the well and carted to the hen house. Of course, from the well to the hen house was up hill both ways, (as my father used to say when describing his trek to school in the old days) in the heat of a North Carolina summer. Rudyard Kipling's Gunga Din knew nothing about hauling water! I could have taught him a thing or two! Chicks also eat constantly. The more they eat, the faster and fatter they grow, so the smart *chickenmeister* makes sure there is light in the hen house at all times. We hung a kerosene lamp high up in the ceiling. If there is light, you can fool chicks into believing it is still day. They will sacrifice sleep and eat day and night. My constitution is similar; I must have some chicken in me. All their eating and drinking tends to produce inordinate amounts of droppings per chick. Multiply by five hundred and you have the makings of a full time shoveling career. It had to be shoveled, put into a wheelbarrow and carted down behind the tobacco barn. Once dumped, it was back for the next load. This is heavy responsibility for a little kid! No one thought so except me. I soon gave up giving them names and treating them like pets. They were indeed, products. I wanted them out of my life.

Chicks are huddlers and cuddlers. They enjoy the safety and comfort of corners and all try to get in the same one. They climb over each other to squeeze into the best position. I am not sure if they are seeking security or warmth. Darwin's theory kicks in; the strongest survive and the weakest are smothered and stomped to death. I think Sara intended another kind of lesson here. Chicks can catch cold. When a peeper sneezes the entire tiny, yellow ball body shakes. How do you treat a chicken's cold? With no experience with these things, the best thing we could think of to do was use an eyedropper to shoot Vicks nose drops into them. Sara and I partitioned off a section of the hen house. As we picked up each peeper and administered its dose of Vicks, we put the peeper on the other side of the partition. Peepers all look alike. At that age, at least, they do not have personalities. You cannot tell them apart but you want to make sure each one gets his medicine and you do not over-dose any of the little fellows. It worked. We didn't lose more than a few chicks.

As far as personality goes, mature chickens do have a personality. They develop quirks as well as personal likes and dislikes. Sara's tenant farmer kept a disagreeable rooster to service his hens. He had a serious dislike for anyone who was not a member of the farmer's immediate family and he had a special contempt for me. I think he knew I was a northerner. A family's chickens usually roamed freely around

47

the farmhouse and the farm. They were not penned up, as were the peepers. They knew the boundaries of their own turf and rarely wandered away. They responded respectfully and with alacrity to the voice and cry of "Here chickie, here chickie, here chickie, chickee" from the farmer's wife at feeding time. They came running from all directions.

Spike, as we called the rotten rooster, was anything but respectful. He hung around the back door, the door used by me and Sara and Hilary, waiting for us to come or go to the house. At the appearance of one of us, especially me, he flapped wings, crowed a nasty little crow, raced toward me in a half run, half fly, and rammed his claw into my leg then took off across the adjacent field crowing in malicious triumph. I was learning to hate chickens and roosters in particular. I left a large stick at the back door and picked it up each time I left the house. I jousted with that miserable rooster every day of the summer. More than once I suggested him as the main entrée for Sunday dinner.

It was late evening in July when Sara roused me out of bed and told me to get dressed. When I got down stairs, she was there with a shotgun in one hand and a rifle in the other. She handed me the rifle and we headed down the hill to the chicken coop. She suspected someone of stealing our chickens. The moon rising over the mountain gave a blue haze to the mild clear star filled night. The dark outlines of building, trees and, rows and rows of tobacco, and smoke rising from the dozens of tobacco curing barns, broke the night into poignant landscapes. Rather than enjoy the beauty of a summer night sprawled out in the Blue Ridge Mountains, I was concerned about the stalking night things like snakes and scary little nocturnal animals crawling about. If one touched me, I was certain I would howl a chilling howl and take off for the house at a speed exceeding the rotation of the earth. For the moment, I clung tightly to Sara.

We blew out the kerosene lamp and sat in the dark on an overturned aluminum washtub in the chicken house. I wanted to run but remained frozen. Sara sat with shotgun at the ready and looking out the back window of the coop. My rifle was pointed out the side window. It was a warm evening, but I was shivering. Was I going to shoot someone who happened to poke his head in the window? Would I spend the rest of my life in jail for murder? I was too young to go to jail. I had heard about the prisoner chain gangs working on the North Carolina roads. The last time we went into Martinsville we saw a group of them in striped work-suits and carrying shovels. They dug trenches at the side of the road. A guard with a rife stood over them and shouted obscenities.

They were hot, sweaty and angry looking. I was sure if they got loose from their chains they would not hesitate to kill the guards and anyone else who happened to be in the way, including me.

Would the chicken thief shoot me first? I was terrified. The chicks carried on a steady chatter of peeping. Chicks are never quiet when people are around. I wondered if the chicken thief would hear the noises from within the coop and decide against a break-in tonight. Sara was sitting quietly listening for any sound. I remembered that her hearing was faulty. My terror intensified as I realized that I was sitting here with a deaf woman who was depending on me to define the night noises and recognize the commotion that was a chicken thief. The rustle of every leaf sent a shock of panic through my veins. I could not breathe nor could I get out from under the crushing weight on my chest. The thudding of pulse in my head tangled the internal and external jangle of the scene. What was real, what wasn't?

We sat this way for at least half an hour then Sara started to giggle. The absurdity of the scene got to her. Although I knew not why, perhaps it was nervousness. I joined in the giggling. Were we really going to shoot someone? We left the chicken house, fired a shot apiece into the air, and went home to bed. The next morning, the countryside was abuzz about the shots heard last night. Sara was quick to spread the word that she had shot at someone trying to steal her chickens. After that, we did not worry about chicken thieves.

What started out, as a project for two little girls soon became a one little girl operation. As I mentioned earlier, Hilary was sickly. Baby chicks made her *more sickly*. She wasn't strong enough to haul water, fill feed trays, or shovel droppings. The odor of chicks and chicken houses made her throw up. If she wasn't throwing up, she had a headache. I sometimes resorted to sticking my finger down my throat in an effort to force myself to throw up but what worked for her just made me sicker.

The chicken experience taught me several things. I learned it is tough to go swimming or play with your friends because chicks need you most of the day. For those children who complain of being bored or having nothing to do, I suggest they try raising chickens. I learned too, you couldn't gauge your fortune in purely mathematical terms. In other words, it does not work if you calculate your profit by multiplying five hundred chicks by fifty cents and expect a profit of two hundred and fifty dollars raising chickens. Things happen. Life happens! You may think you can plot out your life but life gets in the way. There is much wisdom in the adage, "Do not count your chickens before they get to market." This was a great disappointment to me as I had counted on buying a new bicycle with my earnings.

I learned, as did Hercules in the stable, the more crap you shovel, the more you must shovel. But you must keep shoveling or one day it will bury you. I learned it is not a good idea to depend on other people. They have their own agenda. I learned that raising chickens for fun and profit was not much of either. I learned that a shot in the air in the dark is worth two in the hide of a stranger.

I am not sure what Hilary learned. She may have learned that being sickly has its up side. People fuss over you if you are sickly. If your mother is the lady of the manor, they are especially solicitous. The ladies of the hamlet compete to bake cakes and goodies for you. The farmer with the new colt will suggest you might like a horseback ride in a few months. I guess you learn to expect the courtesies given to the privileged. I learned I was not among the privileged. However, I think I got the better education. I was learning to love Sara and see that we had a great time together.

At least once a summer, Sara's mother, Miss Lucy, came to visit. She and Mr. Tom divorced many years before he died. He went to live with the other family he was raising. I did not know Mr. Tom. However, I am told every woman in the county was in love with him. Miss Lucy stayed three weeks and made music all day and well into the night. She plucked away at an old banjo, stomped her foot to keep time, and sang along with her banjo. Looking back, Sara was the only one of her children who was not musical. Most of them played an instrument and sang. One of her daughters had an operatic voice. She was the chief soloist and hymn composer for her church. Miss Lucy taught me to love *shit kicking mountain music.* Her songs spoke of the sorrow of lost loves and the joys of finding new love. They were sad songs, but she made them happy through the twinkle in her eye when she sang and the smile escaping from the corner of her mouth. She had an old RCA record player with music recorded on circular tubes instead of the flat platters, which I knew. She teased that it was a present from Thomas Edison himself. It had to be rewound for each tune played.

On one tube, there was a recording of Enrico Caruso singing *Pagliacci*. It made me cry. In third grade history, I learned about Edison, the Wizard of Menlo Park. Listening to the recording gave me a sense of being in touch with a great

American. Although it was scratchy, I played it repeatedly until Sara screamed and turned it off. Miss Lucy is the closest I came to a grandmother. On summer afternoons, we sat in the double swing chair on the front porch of Sara's house and talked. She played her banjo and told stories of growing up in Stokes Pines. Her poverty made me feel rich by comparison. The floor of their house was dirt. Saturday night bath was taken in an aluminum stand free round washtub set up in the kitchen. They heated buckets of water on the wood fired stove in the kitchen and poured them into the tub. Her father got the first bath, followed by each of the six children then her mother. There was no change of water in between baths. No one was allowed to pee in the tub. Winter mornings were cold for there was a fire in only one room, the kitchen. Most cold nights everyone slept in his long john underwear and a sweater or two. In the morning you took your clothing and ran to the kitchen, put your things on the stove to warm. Everyone dressed huddled around the wood stove. She left school in the third grade because she was needed at home to help care for the *young 'uns*. She told of stealing eggs from the neighbor's hens to buy candy. Stealing eggs sounded like fun and quitting school was not so bad either. However, eight on a bath I could do without. Her music was her lifesaver.

Mr. Tom came along and asked her to marry him. She was beguiled by his henna red hair, handlebar mustache, and strong, determined jaw. He was a sharecropper but had a resolve to own his own farm. His magnetism was irresistible. She packed her banjo and left home. The marriage produced eight children but the life of a charismatic salesman on the road most of the year led to infidelities and eventual divorce. Sara was her father's daughter but the others were all Miss Lucy. She lived to be over ninety and never stopped playing her banjo.

Five

In the fall, it was back to New York, school, Washington Heights and the Automat. Dad and I did not last long with Sara and Hilary. Sara and Dad were diligently bogged down in weekly sometimes daily, arguments. It seemed to happen when there was too much rye whiskey around. Dad was not much of a drinker but Sara loved high balls. I don't know what they argued about except that money and marriage were often mentioned. Dad didn't have enough money, and Sara thought he should get a divorce so they could marry. Dad liked his life style. He had no ties and few responsibilities. He was free of the tedium of family living, and his free spirit was free to do its thing. Married but separated from his wife gave Dad a perfect shield against becoming permanently entangled in another family.

There was a Christmas when we drove to Richmond, Virginia, from New York with Sara,

56

Hilary, Sara's sister and brother-in-law, their two children and the dog in one car. Each adult had at least one kid on his lap. Dad called us "Poor white trash on the move." There was a new baby in Sara's family, so the clan was gathering to celebrate the new arrival and the yuletide. We were there one day when a grotesque argument broke out among the adults. I suspect it had to do with Sara's constant complaint that Dad was not making a move to get a divorce. Several highballs and that was the order of the day. Once an argument started, there were no peacemakers. Everyone got into it. In the end, no one remembered the original issue fought about but each person brought his own agenda with a spouse or with an in-law. The grievances of years were aired on a regular basis. Dad, Sara's brother-in-law, and I headed back to New York on Christmas Eve. We drove through the night and part of the day. Dad and I had Christmas dinner at the Automat.

Christmas was a difficult time for me. My father's many friends frequently invited us for Christmas Day dinner. Often he accepted three or four dinner invitations. This meant we darted from house to house with a meal to be eaten at each home. I would be introduced to the children, play with them for an hour or two, admire their toys and move on to the next house. Dad gave money to each child as a Christmas present.

Sometimes he gave the boys a football or some baseball equipment. I, too, got money as a present with the counsel, "Buy yourself something." He was a generous man and gave me everything he could. However, I minded not getting toys and other presents to open on Christmas morning. I minded not being in my own home on Christmas. As a guest in someone's home, I had to be an adult - Daddy's big girl. I wasn't allowed to be a child in my childhood. I think I was born an adult. Either that or I am destined never to grow up.

Although Dad was usually sober, his hot temper prevented him from calming most arguments. Often the arguments with Sara escalated to the point where I found myself packing my belongings and heading into the night to a boarding house in another part of town and into a new school the next day.

New York was filled with Irish widows and work-at-home Irish wives who rented out rooms with board to gentlemen like my father. These women shared large five or six bedroom apartments with spouses and children until the children were married and moved into their own large apartments. The wives supplemented the meager wages of their husbands by taking in boarders. The widows supported themselves by renting rooms. While the Irish women were providing room and board, the Italian women of New York City were running hole in the wall pasta and pizza places with their husbands and scrimping their pennies together to buy Manhattan brownstones. The new world, particularly New York City, was the land of opportunity for these recent immigrants.

Dad and I were boarding house hoppers - a week in one, a month in another, three months in another. In between times, it would be back to Sara's apartment and out again with another row. Lucky for me we usually managed to get back to Sara's just in time for me to go to North Carolina for the summer. The farm was the one constant in my life.

I don't remember any other children in the boarding houses. I don't remember seeing anyone except men and the nice ladies who ran them. I don't remember talking to anyone or anyone talking to me. It may have been because I was too shy to talk to anyone, because Dad told me not to talk to strangers, or because everyone was too busy. Each person was very busy working, trying to eke out a living. Residents got up in the morning, had breakfast, and were off to work. They returned for a six-thirty dinner, which they ate in common and went to their rooms or went out for the evening. Besides the woman who ran the business, there were never women in these boarding houses. It seems women who were not married lived at home but single or divorced men had the privilege of living on their own. I did not have meals with them. No one told me but I think I was not supposed to be there. A boarding house was for working adults. Children were not welcome. Dad probably sweet-talked the Irish ladies into taking me in. My job was to be invisible. I ate three meals a day at the Automat.

Dad was usually asleep when I got up to go to school. He worked nights and met friends after work. He came home about midnight. I got dressed, took my schoolbooks, and went to the Automat for breakfast. Sometimes Dad would meet me for lunch, and we both went to the Automat. If he joined me, that was special. I got anything I wanted including a trip to the candy store. Across the street from every school, there was a "mom and pop" candy store. For ten cents, you were treated to ten different kinds of candy. Any kid who showed up for class after lunch with a pocketful of penny candy was a hero. You could store up on pencils, pens, paper, notebooks, three ring binders and everything you needed for class at the candy store. But the best thing about the candy store was the ice cream sodas they made. Dad and I sat up at the soda fountain and order a black and white - chocolate ice cream and vanilla syrup. They came in those tall glasses and with long narrow spoons. The glasses were narrow on the bottom. You had to dig your spoon down to get the thick syrup that lodged down there. That was the sweetest part.

After school, I regularly went to Woolworth's Five and Ten Cent store, which was across the street from the Automat. I could kill an hour and a half before deciding how to spend the quarter Dad gave me at lunchtime. Doll clothes and cheap perfume were favorite purchases. Every doll I owned was named Emily. I remember talking to my dolls a whole lot. Emily drank water and frequently needed her diaper changed. I was forever washing and drying diapers!

Five o'clock dinner at the Automat, home for homework and bed was the drill. I wonder what my homework papers looked like in the morning when I got to school. I remember ripping out sheet after sheet of loose-leaf, rolling it into a ball and tossing it into a wastebasket. I would do almost anything to get out of doing homework.

I ordinarily did not hear Dad come in. Moving from boarding house to boarding house and from Sara's to boarding house was my life from about the age of seven to twelve. I attended six different elementary schools in three states and two boroughs of New York City. I do not have any old report cards, so I do not know for certain, but I must have been a horrible student. I do remember being terrified that the teacher would ask me to read or to answer a question. It wasn't until I got to high school that I began to enjoy going to school.

There were times when Dad moved out of the boarding house and left me there with the landlady. He never told me where he moved. Looking back, I realize he moved in with a new girlfriend. My father was an extraordinarily handsome man. At six feet tall with hair black as a tinker's pot, he had a winning Irish smile and a personality that poured honey into unsweetened lives. In my early years, I too wanted to marry him.

He was every widow and divorcee's delight. He was soft-spoken, gentle, courteous, and respectful of women and an easy spender. He was available for Sunday dinner with a woman's family as well as Friday and Saturday night dates. He was a special favorite of widows and divorcees with children. Uncle John loved kids and always brought presents. A relationship lasted until the woman started talking about marriage. It was then that Dad would point out that he was married and, therefore not eligible to marry. If she pressed on and suggested he get a divorce, either he terminated the relationship or she realized she was in a no-win situation and she ended things. Sometimes I met these women and sometimes I did not. The one thing about Sara, she was in and out of our lives for twenty years. Over time, she realized that John made a better lover and companion than a husband. She gave up the idea of marriage but never gave up loving him.

Six

I slept very little for the painful thoughts of my childhood broke the night into a series of bad dreams. I realized more than ever Sara's important place in my life. Before going to breakfast, I called Leonard. He slept in the office last night because Whitney was on a rampage. She could not deal with the indignity of him giving up a prestigious position with an esteemed law firm to work for pittance in a struggling real estate office. He was causing undue hurt and financial suffering to her and to their children. He should get over it and do what every other man does – grow up! Happiness be damned! He was too young for a mid-life crisis. She more than suspected the relationship between Leonard and me.

It happened quite innocently. We had worked late. A late December blizzard covered New York with fifteen inches of snow. It was an exceptionally bitter winter with more than forty inches of snow. People were sick to death of below freezing temperatures and the inconvenience of travel around town. LaGuardia and Kennedy airports were closed at least twice a week because of weather conditions. Travelers in and out of the city were becoming accustomed to sleeping on benches and on the floor of the airport. Trains to Westchester were jam packed, and running late. At best, he would arrive home in time to shower, change clothing, and travel back to the city. It did not make sense.

We bought a bottle of wine and walked uptown to my apartment. No traffic moved. Snow lowers a hush on the city like nothing else. The usual rush of cars, taxicabs, and trucks dashing to beat the red light at the corner, winds to a standstill. The sounds of horns are muted, in respect for the sacredness of snow. It is a time when the city is safest as criminals put off until tomorrow what they planned to do today. There was only the lonely wail of a fire engine fighting through snowdrifts. Tomorrow's newspaper will fill with the news of a family who lost everything because weather delayed the arrival of firemen. It is always like that.

We drank a glass of wine and then another, unmindful of anything in the evening except ourselves. Was it the wine, or the enchantment of snow? There is a great tenderness in first desire. We braided into each other. My world filled with the sweetness of wild strawberries. I was transported back to the early flush of passion as a college student when Leonard and I first made love; when the world stood still; when we were the only two people alive; when there was no Whitney. Was it possible to regain those days? Can we undo the past? I had long since gotten over being angry with him for leaving me. I shrugged it off as what I deserved. After all, the rest of my life taught me that Murphy was an optimist with his law of the universe.

Our evenings together became more frequent. He spent more and more nights in the city and fewer in Westchester. It wasn't long before Leonard decided he wanted a divorce. She could keep the house and they would share custody of the children. He never really was in love with Whitney. It was over!

Putty startled me out of my musings when she came to my bedroom door with a cup of coffee and the suggestion that we get started to Taylorsville. Everyone else was up and out already. She chided my late sleeping habits (it was eight o'clock), as evidence of my decadent city life style. I dressed quickly and we took off. We got to the hospital about ten o'clock. Sara was in intensive care and had tubes and needles protruding from everywhere. She was very weak but smiled when she saw us. We made small talk, lied, and, told her she looked wonderful. I was shocked at how thin she was. Her hair had returned to its natural gray. She was without makeup and was disheveled looking. I took out a hairbrush and rearranged her hair. Then I applied powder and lipstick to her face. She never appeared in public without full makeup and coiffed hair. As sick as she was she appreciated looking better for her public. It was a small thing I could do to make her more comfortable.

The nursing staff was over worked. There were not enough rooms to accommodate all patients. The town had grown so fast the medical establishment was not able to keep up. Many patients were on gurneys in the hall waiting for someone to give up a space. There were portable intravenous drips dangling everywhere. Nurses and doctors treated people in the corridor. Family members hovered around hurling angry quips at hospital staff. They were frustrated with what appeared to be hospital neglect of their sick loved one. It was hot and the un-air-conditioned halls made folks testy and impatient.

Putty, mother of five, was a better nurse than I so she tended to Sara's needs while I concentrated on looking for Sara's family, or what was left of it. With my cell phone, I was able to make contact with Harry and he promised to be in touch with the other family members. No, he did not know where to find Hilary. As far as anyone knew, she married at seventeen, and went north. Since the fan magazines never mentioned her name, it was assumed she was not a big Hollywood star. She broke Sara's heart. They fought and finally lost contact. Putty's view was that Sara had tried too hard to please her spoiled daughter. Hilary was Sara's life yet her ungrateful and selfish daughter resented her mother. She was ashamed of Sara for a lifestyle she thought unacceptable in genteel society. Putty and I however, loved Sara and were grateful for all she did to make our miserable childhoods tolerable. She was good to us.

Sara drifted in and out of consciousness several times during the day. We kept talking to her in the hope that she could hear us. We talked about the old days when we were children. We reminded her of how good she was to us and how much we loved her. Putty remembered Sara making dresses for her and giving her shoes to wear to school. One year she bought her a winter coat and a scarf. I reminded of the many summers on the farm and the good times we had. It was Sara who made Putty's and my childhoods memorable. We cried and laughed and prayed she would get well. We sensed she was engaged in her last debate with God. It was a penumbra moment when death, the rude intruder, was echoed in the cheery platitudes of the hospital staff monitoring the miracles of modern medical technology.

Evening approached. A light rain spackled the window and ran down the pane in tiny rivers. Taylorville's tepid landscape was settling down for another non-descript night. Putty had to leave to get dinner for the children. Ethan was good for peanut butter and jelly sandwiches but dinner was beyond his talent. The nightly bath, a bedtime story, and last minute glasses of water were tasks for two. Putty would be back in the morning.

They rolled in a cot and I settled in as night nurse. Tired as I was, I could not sleep. I wanted to tell Sara all the things I neglected to tell her these many years. I wanted to tell her about Leonard. Of all people, she would understand. Instead, I talked to her about my life as a boarding house kid when she and dad were feuding. Strange how we leave the important things unsaid to the people we love then hope for the blessing of time to get it done lest we carry the baggage of grief the rest of our days. I remembered the difficult days of Dad's funeral.

Seven

Leonard insisted on coming with me. We drove to Forty-second Street and entered the darkened mouth of the Lincoln Tunnel. I have never been comfortable heading into the bowel of the under river route to New Jersey. My mind's eye sees cracks in the wall and I imagine millions of tons of Hudson River water rushing in on me. My head pounds and my heart stops as the burst of water completely chokes off all air to my lungs and bashes my car against the fissured walls. One of these days, I shall not make it out to the top of the Weehawken Palisades. Carbon monoxide fills the car despite closed windows. What chance does a Volkswagen Passad have against sixteen wheelers on three sides? It is the pit of the damned eliminating light and air replacing it with the chaos of roaring sound and blackness that sticks to the lining of your soul I was happy for Leonard's presence both to get me through the tunnel and to be with me when we got to Mazarrini's Funeral Home. I did not know what viper's nest I was approaching. The telephone call from Kyle Reilly, a colleague of Dad at the print shop, said only that dad was being waked here in New Jersey. He thought I should know dad had not survived a massive heart attack.

Two somber young men, in black suits and black ties directed us upstairs and down the hall to the right. I signed the book on the podium just inside the door and looked around for a face I knew. Leonard and I made our way through the sea of black-garbed strangers and knelt down at the casket in the front of the room. It was Dad. I had difficulty reckoning with the idea that I was gazing on the dead body of my father. It was all so sudden; so unexpected.

There are no windows in rooms we wake the dead. There is instead the light and air of deception. The pallid ashen face of the dead is lit to reflect our theory of eternity; there is no death. The sweet odor of flowers hangs on from one waked body to the next. We dare not inhale the truth of decay. I was unprepared for grief. It came so suddenly and without warning. I looked down at my father and wished he would come to life if only for a minute or two. I wanted to read his eyes, to feel his body heat, to tell him I loved him, to say goodbye. I wanted more time to make up for the years we spent hurting each other. Do people leave when they wish? Do they not want to say goodbye? But it is over. Memory is all the future can boast.

I leaned over and kissed Dad's forehead. It was cold and without the resilience I remember from the days when as a child he hugged and cuddled me. Leonard grabbed my arm to steady me. I wanted to scream in rage and anguish but that is not acceptable. I tarried a few minute on my knees to gain composure before I was ready to face the other people in the room.

The room was so crowded, people talked over other people and carried on two conversations at the same time jostling to stay in proximity to the person they were addressing. It was the kind of small talk to which no one pays attention but it is what is expected and it is kept light and meaningless. Old friends and distant relatives show up. Some to gloat that the old goat finally got his; some to visit with people they have not seen for ages; some to gossip; some to resurrect old feuds and some to mourn.

The mandatory "black" was everywhere. Men wore black suits. Women wore black dress, black stockings and black shoes as well as black veils over their heads. Little children were in black. I was out of place in a navy blue tailored dress. I looked around for a familiar face but saw only strangers. Could this be happening? It was surreal. Was that my father among this band of strangers? It was then I caught a glimpse of Marty Flynn heading toward me from across the room. His face was drawn and pained. He did not look pleased to see me. Marty and Dad had been friends for at least thirty years. In the old days when they were playing the numbers and the horses, he and Dad were runners for the bookies. At one point they even were in business for themselves. A few major "hits" and they were back to being runners. Since Dad did not drive, Marty took him everywhere he had to go. Dad worked at night and Marty's employment was of dubious nature, they met at the diner each morning for breakfast and to scope out the horses for the day.

"Who are all these people? I don't know any of them."

"Most of them are Johnny's wife's family." To his friends Dad was always "Johnny."

"That's his widow over there."

Across the room sitting in an upholstered red velvet wing-backed queen ann chair I gazed on a woman of about seventy with salon coiffed blue gray hair. She stood to greet a guest. I could see that she was quite tall, almost six feet. There was a black lace scarf gracefully draped over her head and shoulders. She was an elegant woman, the kind my father would have adored. The problem was Dad had the Irish irrational dislike for Italians. I could not imagine he married one.

Standing to her right were three women in their late thirties or early forties. Their striking resemblance to each other and to her strongly suggested they had to be her daughters. Their eyes were swollen red and moist with deep rings of tears. I turned to Marty, my eyes burning with disbelief and exploding with questions.

"They got married about seven months ago. You were not supposed to know."

"How can this be? He is still married to Alice!"

"I don't know anything about Alice. I do know he is married because I was there in City Hall with them. As a matter of fact, I was his best man."

Droplets of water ran down my neck and into my bra. The heat of the room, the overpowering scent of roses and lilies and chrysanthemums, the news of my new stepfamily drizzled all energy out of me. I slumped into Leonard's arms.

Eight

There is only one landlady I can put a name on and almost a face. We had a room in Mrs. Ryan's boarding house at a time when Dad needed to move out and did not have much cash. He could not afford to live with a new girlfriend, pay his share of expenses, and pay full freight for me at Mrs. Ryan's. It was agreed that I would sleep on a cot in Mrs. Ryan's own bedroom and eat my meals at her kitchen table. I was not permitted in the dining room with the other boarders. I remember Mrs. Ryan as a kindly motherly woman. She was a widow with one son who attended the Catholic elementary school of the parish. Mrs. Ryan was appalled that I was nine years old; supposedly, a Catholic yet did not attend Church and had not received my First Communion. She instructed my father that if I were to live under her roof, I would attend Church and I would go to after-school instructions and receive First Communion. She was also appalled that I sporadically attended the Methodist Church during the summer. She was convinced somebody was going to hell for allowing a Catholic child to worship the false gods of the Protestant Church! I had a feeling I was the one going to Hell. I began to fear for my father as well. I had enough guilt for both of us. Mrs. Ryan was a no-nonsense woman who knew what was what with God. I began to fear for Sara too for she rarely attended even the Protestant Church. However, on thinking it over I decided she might be better off that way since the Methodist Church could not guarantee that folks were going to heaven and might even be insuring hell.

I made my First Communion with a group of seven-year-old children. Finding the traditional white dress for a nine year old chubby was not easy. My Aunt Mary, Dad's sister took me to a shop in Brooklyn where we found an almost perfect fit. The *chubbies* of the world go through life with ill fitting, often *mature looking* clothing. During most of my childhood, I looked like a forty-year-old midget. Learning to feel ugly is easy. Once ugliness is learned it is a formidable task to be rid of the concept. No matter how often you are told, it is not so, this image of yourself is indelibly ground into your identity. It is who you are.

"Who made you?"
"God made me."
"Why did God make you?"

"God made me to know Him and love Him in this life and be happy with Him in heaven."

It was my first exposure to the Baltimore Catechism, the working religious text for all Catholic children. The studious child memorized each question and each answer in the book. When called upon, you stood, Sister asked the question and the student was expected to spout the answer exactly as it was written in the Catechism. Generations of Catholics learned their faith in this fashion. Perhaps it is because while wrestling with the Catechism, we had little or no understanding of the dogma contained in the Catechism that so many Catholics never got beyond this rote regurgitation to a mature understanding of their faith. On the other hand, I have heard Catholics lament the system of their youth and condemn the present method of teaching to understand the concepts of the religion and expressing it in there own terms.

I have never been a fan of rote memory. While classmates memorize the entire Catechism, and reams, and reams of lines of poetry, I am barely able to memorize my telephone number. My public school head, accustomed to knowing the why of things, floundered, and fluffed through six months of religious instruction. Finally, through the generosity and patience of Sister Mary of the Baltimore Catechism, I mastered enough of the tenets of the Church to make first communion with my class.

I walked up to the altar, opened my mouth, and allowed the priest to place the Host on my tongue. I remember feeling, "What's the big deal?" I guess I expected the earth to tremble when God came into my body. Sister Mary of the Baltimore Catechism promised more! I was disappointed. After Mass, Aunt Mary gave me a large bouquet of white carnation. Dad took us all, including Mrs. Ryan and her son, to Bickfords for breakfast.

Not only was I ugly, I was stupid. The only hope for me was to develop a sense of humor. Everybody loves the class clown. As the tallest one in the First Communion group, I was the last one in the procession. Today, at five feet three inches, and shrinking, I am usually the first in any line-up. I think it was one of the first times I realized I was always out of step with the rest of the world. I operate in *lag time* - always behind the rest of the world; I get to the normal things later than everyone else in the world; I come late to the dance.

In school, I was always in the wrong class for my age. It seems each time I changed schools they put me back a grade. For many semesters, I was in a bridge class. A bridge class is composed of the smarter kids from a lower grade and the slower kids from the next grade. A class with second and third grade students would be a bridge class, or a class composed of third and fourth graders would be a bridge class. A second grade student in a bridge class would go to the fourth grade the following year. In this way, schools would try to get a student on grade level or seek to advance a student with potential. I was aiming at getting on grade level.

I was always the new kid in the class. While other kids spent most of their lives in the same neighborhood, I lived in many neighborhoods. There is no one I grew up with, nor are there any life long friends from my early childhood except those in Stokes Pines. It wasn't until high school that I was able to make friends. Without a neighborhood to call your own, nor a permanent home, nor long-term friends nor family - brothers, sisters, aunts and uncles, grandparents - one gets a sense of not belonging. One is rootless and out of step with the world. I never felt I belonged anyplace. There is more than one kind of homelessness. Homeless is a state of mind as well as a physical condition.

The lifestyle of my childhood taught me the importance of rituals, the symbols of belonging. They are the tethers, which ground us. They provide us with identity. I watched from the periphery as families shared with us their rituals of family meals, religious and national holidays, birthdays, graduations, family outings, and vacations. Not every ritual was accomplished without disagreements and sometimes a feud or two. But in every case, everyone developed the understanding that he belonged. Someone described home as "The

place, when you have to go there, they have to take you in." I guess that is because you belong. James Patterson has the right idea about family and the important things in life. If you miss any of them, your life lacks balance. For Patterson, life is a game in which you juggle work, family, health, friends, and integrity. In a balanced life, the only ball you can afford to drop is work. It took me many years to learn this.

Nine

The closest I came to a childhood home was Sara's Stokes Pines farm. Summers were free and fun. Sara designed the house and set it on two of the fifteen acres of her farm, then enclosed it with a white picket fence. The house was a red brick colonial with white shutters and white trim. It was positioned on a small knoll high enough to be seen and envied by most of the farmhouses in the area, which were in various degrees of disrepair. There was a small bathroom on the second floor, the only indoor bathroom in the county until about nineteen hundred fifty-five. It was installed in anticipation of electricity coming to Stokes Pines. For flushing and for baths we carried water from the well on the front lawn to the bathroom. We were three on a tub rather than the eight on a tub in Miss Lucy's day. Hauling water in the heat of a North Carolina summer was exhausting. This city girl learned to do a major part of her peeing and more serious business outdoors behind the barn or deep in the woods at the back of the main house despite the ants and crawly things romping around in the grass. The trauma remains in my psyche to this day. To this day, when I travel my concern is not the comfort of the hotel bed but the luxuriousness of the bathroom.

The first time local folks came to see Sara's new house, the bathroom was the first room shown and the one that interested people most. After all, if you have seen one living room, you have seen them all but an indoor bathroom was worth investigating. Sara was the envy of the community.

The sunroom just off the living room had three walls of glass and an inside wall with a ceiling to floor bookcase. The dark window shades remained closed all day to protect against the heat of the summer sun. The bookcase was filled with musty, yellow paged, ancient books, which looked as though they had never been read. One book I enjoyed reading and read it over, and over, and over -Tro*pic of Cancer*, by Henry Miller. Putty, Millie, and I could not believe such things! We took it off the shelf and slightly moved the other books so the empty space would not be so noticeable if Sara happened along. We wiled away summer afternoons down behind the hen house enjoying the heat of the day and the heat of the book. Our bodies experienced a strange tingling and at times the most exquisite joy. We giggled a lot and rolled around in the tall grass. I began to see Jake in a different light. I imagined us undressing each other.

A long fieldstone walkway extended from the front porch to the road. The walkway was lined with a boxwood hedge. There were two umbrella trees, one on either side of the walkway. Their branches and leaves were so heavy and tight together that I wondered how rain got through them to refresh their roots. They were a haven for birds during summer storms. I knew when a storm was about to descend by the close harmony of every variety of southern bird as all scuffled for a position of safety. It was time to close all the windows in the house; put the garden tool in the shed and make sure Molly was safe in the stable.

I had my own bedroom. It had two windows and a walk-in closet larger than some of the furnished rooms in which Dad and I lived. That was my secret place. I took books and dolls in there. I read to myself and I read to the dolls. A horsehide child's rocking horse was stored there. It stood nearly five feet tall. As it was the last present her father gave her, it was Hilary's prize toy. Understandably, she was very possessive about it. However, she never sat on it or looked at it. Nevertheless, I, as well as all others was forbidden to go near it. Well, she should have put it in *her* closet if she didn't want me to ride it! I was an avid horsewoman. My friends, Millie, Putty, Jake, and I played *Wild West Rodeo* when we were sure Hilary was not in the house.

The nearly two acres of front and back lawn required serious attention each week. It fell to my lot to be the chief manicurist. Sometimes I managed to convince one or two of the neighbor kids as well as Putty and Jake, to help me on the promise that I would talk Sara into driving us all to the river for a swim. However, my real champion was Uncle Harry. As I said, he was a *tinkerer* and an inventor. We had three old hand lawn mowers that he strung together- one overlapping the other so that instead of mowing a row eighteen inches wide at a time I was able to mow a row fifty-four inches wide. He borrowed a cross bar from an old plow, hooked the lawn mowers to it then attached that to the harness on Molly, our brown and white pinto horse. I followed behind Molly. I learned to juggle the reins attached to Molly and at the same time keep the three lawn mowers on track. However, there were two slight drawbacks to this system. Molly was careless about her hygiene habits and frequently laid dung down in front of the mowers. I was not able to get out of the way quickly enough before the blades picked up her droppings and churned them out behind. At times, my arms and clothing were caught in the spew and I ran into the house crying and cursing Molly.

The other problem with mowing the lawn in this manner was the discovery of poison oak and poison ivy growing close to the white picket fence enclosing the lawn. There was an uncultivated field on the other side of the fence through which weeds and foliage of every pedigree trespassed on to my beautiful lawn. The sap from the poison oak splashed on to me and I broke out in a full body rash of runny sores. It even got into my eyes and ears. It was then, I decided horticulture was a career I could eliminate from my list of things to do with my life. Except for these two minor problems, Molly and I looked forward to the weekly chore. The lawn was mowed in a third of the time. Harry was my hero!

Molly was a beautifully marked brown and white pinto horse Sara kept because she wanted Hilary to learn to ride. All the best people in New York rode horseback in Central Park. Despite the fashionable jodhpurs, riding cap and riding crop, Hillary was not the least bit interested in horseback riding. I rode Molly the mile and a half to the post office every day, then through the backfield to get fresh milk and butter from the farmer. Some afternoons Putty, Jake, Millie and I climbed on Molly and went exploring. We covered the countryside looking for strange and interesting places. We found a cave that was large enough for us to ride into on Molly. It is surprising how brave you can be in a dark unknown place if you travel on a horse capable of returning you to safety at a gallop. Since I was the sissy and the city kid, I got to sit in the saddle while the others fended for themselves behind me. Besides, it was my turf. I could call the shots.

One morning Molly was not interested in our morning chores. We got out of the stable and down to the front gate when she took off at a gallop back to of the stable. She paid no attention to my calls of "whoa! Whoa! I pulled the reign as hard as I could but she was unstoppable until she hit the piece of barbed wire stretched from one pole to another blocking the entrance to the stable. The barbed wire ripped into her chest. She stopped short and I went flying over her head and on to the ground. I looked up to see four hoofs crossing over my head. Molly had the good sense to avoid stepping on me. She went into her stall and I limped back to the house, pride more hurt than body. Sara insisted that I go right back to the stable, get back up on Molly, and complete my chores. "If you don't, you will fear horseback riding for the rest of your life," she said. "Besides, you cannot let molly get away with that." Neither

87

Molly nor I were thrilled with the deal. When she saw me coming she whinnied and stomped about in her stall. I washed out her wound and put a bandage over it. Off we went to the post office.

The house was furnished with oriental rugs, Royal Doulton China, and Waterford glassware, all of which Sara purchased in New York and transported via flivver to this rural back woods hamlet. There was a ten foot stuffed sailfish hanging over the fireplace. Benedict landed it during one of his fishing trips to the Bahamas. The locals were in awe of the house and its furnishings. Sara enjoyed her role as the hometown girl who made good. Flaunting it was part of the fun. She brought New York friends and business associates to Stokes Pines for long weekend junkets or short vacations. They partied, hunted, fished, and caroused into the night and thought it was life on the farm. Sleeping arrangements were always interesting. Hilary and I were sent to the couches in the basement. People who arrived together often did not sleep together.

North Carolina is a dry State. Several days before a party, Sara and I took a trip deep into the back hills to see *big ole Black Uncle Cyrus*. The road to Uncle Cyrus' house was hardly a road at all. It was an unpaved path with tall grass beaten down by the passage of horse drawn wagons Uncle Cyrus used to haul tobacco, grains and the family rations of food as well take the family to church. The path was also beaten down by the cars his customers drove when they came to purchase his money crop. Uncle Cyrus was the best maker of *moonshine* in the county. Since *the Law* was always on the lookout for illegal stills, the visit to Uncle Cyrus was top secret. It seemed everyone knew where to find the still but it was only when there was pressure from the Ladies Temperance Society of the Methodist Church, was Uncle Cyrus temporarily put out of business. He moved the still a few yards upstream on the same creek and was back in business before *The Law* had time to file its report.

Sara insisted on a tasting before she bought a case of moonshine. Day old moonshine was not acceptable. It had to be aged at least two weeks to meet her standards. Uncle Cyrus brought out three glasses. He was proud of his *likker*. I took one sip then spewed it out of my mouth. It tasted like rubbing alcohol and felt as though my mouth was engulfed in fire. For a few seconds I could not breathe. I understood why the Indians called the white man's drink "fire water." However, Sara's guests who consumed it in great quantities before they passed out did not find it distasteful.

Frog hunting was a favorite hunt. Fried in olive oil and garlic, frog legs was a great delicacy.

There was a large marshy pond a few miles from the farm. It had a tremendous frog population. Sara, her guests I and waited until after dark then boarded flat bottom rowboats and, with rifles, searched out frogs. We listened for the "ribitt, ribitt" then shone a flashlight where we heard the call of the frog, took aim and shot, hoping to hit only the upper part of the frog's torso. A shot through the eye caused the frog to leap several feet out of the water. If you are quick with the long handled net, you can retrieve the frog before it falls back into the pond. It takes a heap of frogs to make a feast for twenty people. We lacquered the night with the sounds of gunshot. One night, Sam Holtzman, a frequent partier at the farm, tried to take himself, from the stern, to the bow, of the boat. His legs, wobbly with moonshine, gave out and he tumbled into the marshy water. The water was a mere three feet deep but he almost drowned. We got him home and to the amusement of all, he spent the rest of the evening in one of Sara's dressing gowns.

At the time, I thought frog hunting was great fun and great sport. I was fascinated with aiming and shooting a rifle. Today I realize it is not fun and certainly not sport. The frog did not have a chance. You shot at it from no more than five feet away. When there were enough frogs to feast all the guests, we headed home to clean, fry, and consume the kill and more moonshine.

Learning to kill your food was part of the culture. There was no sentimentality about the food chain. Sara insisted that I experience the southern farm girl's rite of passage to womanhood. For some reason, Hilary was exempt from these things - and from hunting or from stalking chicken thieves. The farmers lived on the native animals - rabbits, squirrels, possum, as well as hogs and chicken. There was no beef as it was too expensive and, without refrigeration, it was difficult to store. Every farmer raised hogs, which he slaughtered in the fall. The pork was heavily salted, smoked, and stored in a cement casing set in the creek that flowed close to every house. Thick fatty bacon and fatty pork were eaten all year around. Bacon was put into, cooked and canned with the hundreds and hundreds of pounds of string beans consumed each year. The men were the main hunters of rabbits, squirrels, and possum but every woman was expected to do her share of the hunting. When the men were too busy in the field to hunt for the family dinner, the women picked up the rife and went into the woods. If a woman did not come back with a rabbit or squirrel, there was no meat for dinner. Women had total responsibility for raising and slaughtering chicken, the mainstay of the diet. There were chickens running loose on every farm. If there was to be chicken for dinner, the woman selected a chicken captured it, wrung its neck, plucked and fried it. Sara insisted that I experience this custom. Many times, I witnessed this but never once did, I imagine I would be asked to do it. However, Sara considered it part of my education.

Sara selected the chicken she wanted for dinner, I chased it down and took it to the woodshed behind the house. To wring the chicken's neck, I held the body in one hand. With the other hand, I grasped the neck near the head. Meanwhile a chicken eye was looking up at me wondering what was happening. I was shaking. Sara had invited several neighbor women to witness my initiation. My heart rate was at the speed of light. It was too late to turn back. Any show of weakness, would condemn me to be viewed, as a weak baby not a maturing young woman of twelve, a soft spoiled New Yorker. It was my first real game of *chicken!* When I was ready, I tossed the body of the chicken in the air, hanging on to the head and neck. At the same time, I twisted the neck and broke it. When I let go of the chicken, it leapt about for several minutes with its broken neck and it died. I had prepared a bucket of boiling water ready to plunge the chicken in to loosen the feathers so it would be more easily plucked. After that, cleaning out the insides and preparing the chicken for frying was easy. The women cheered. For days, Sara touted my prowess and womanhood throughout the countryside. For weeks, the women of the community celebrated my feat.

Northern city girls become women at the onset of their menstrual period. Mine arrived when I killed a chicken! There is not much dignity in that. I was embarrassed and grief stricken. It was a horrendous experience. I shall never forget that chicken eye looking at me. I did it once but will never do it again. Sara did it each time she served chicken. At dinner that night and for many nights afterwards, I was unable to eat anything but vegetables and I hated vegetables. I was all right with rabbits and squirrels but I would not hunt them again either for I am too much of a city girl. However, I have enormous respect and admiration for the farmers who do the dirty work that provides the rest of us the luxury of our meat and potatoes.

When breaded and fried, rabbit, squirrel, and possum all taste somewhat like chicken. Since both Hilary and I were both squeamish about bunnies and squirrels, Sara mixed in chicken to fool us. It was not hard to sort things out. Rabbit, squirrel tasted gamier, and the legs, everyone's favorite, are smaller.

The premier diet for the poor farmer of the time was corn, tomatoes, snap beans (known in the north as string beans), chicken, and pork.

He raised all of this himself. Every meal all summer was snap beans, tomatoes, and corn. Fried chicken or pork were eaten on Sunday and when there were guests. Squirrel, rabbit, and possum were eaten when men could take time away from tobacco farming to hunt. Breakfast was homemade biscuits and gravy. That was it - seven days a week all summer. Watermelon was a favorite with all the kids. Watermelon tasted best when you stole into a farmer's patch, selected a ripe melon, cracked it open on a nearby rock, and let the juice run down your clothes as you ate. It was warm and more delectable because it was stolen forbidden fruit.

There was plenty of fresh but un-pasteurized milk, butter, and buttermilk. I never learned to drink buttermilk. For me it was a distasteful concoction of sour milk with chunks of butter in it. I did learn to milk a cow, however. Daisy owned the farm across the road. She was widowed with five grown children. Her three older girls were in their thirties and not married, a condition barely acceptable in a society which married women off at age fourteen or fifteen. The three were always invited to Sara's parties.

Daisy had a relationship with her cow that most people reserve for their dogs or their lovers. Jessica was a basic brown and white Guernsey milk cow that produced both white milk and chocolate milk, or so the city kid was told. Each morning Daisy led Jessica from the barn, across the road on to the pasture behind Sara's house. There, Jessica ate her heart out all day. This morning walk was a time for the two of them to discuss the important things in life. Daisy and Jessica talked about suitable husbands for the three daughters. Sometimes, when Daisy returned for Jessica for the evening milking, I coaxed and was allowed to draw Jessica's rich cream. Daisy had to convince Jessica that it was all right for me to do the honors. She missed Daisy's experienced and gentle hands. It was fun to squirt the warm foamy milk directly into my mouth.

It ceaselessly amazed me that in any household a tin of fresh biscuits could be whipped up at a moment's notice. The same was true for corn bread. The flour and cornmeal were out and ready at all times. The corn bread was cooked in an iron frying pan and then flipped upside down on to a steaming hot plate. With lots of butter, it could be an entire meal and often was. In Daisy's kitchen the wood-burning stove was always hot and the cornmeal sat on a special butcher-block table. I created an endless list of excuses why it was necessary for me to visit Daisy. She never disappointed me.

Women's summer work was to can the tomatoes, corn, and snap beans in mason jars so

95

there would be food for the winter. I remember peeling bushels upon bushels of peaches that wound up as preserves on biscuits. The food was good, although monotonous. The fare was different at Sara's house. For one thing, there were frogs' legs as well as steaks and a variety of vegetables.

Tobacco was the money crop for these North Carolina farmers. Like most farming, raising tobacco is labor intensive. It is hot, backbreaking work subject to the whims of suckers (tobacco worms), blights, and weather. It requires the involvement of all members of the family. When a tobacco farmer is *priming*, harvesting the tobacco leaves, the entire neighborhood shows up to help. They are dependent on each other's cooperation to bring in the crop. They are family. In addition to family and neighbors, the help of the local Black day worker was necessary. Day workers worked for a dollar a day. Today migrant workers come up from Mexico each year to bring in the tobacco crop. I was soon conscripted into the work force. Sara thought it was good for me to learn to do manual labor. She would not allow me to be paid for my services so I was a worker in much demand.

In a tobacco community, work, and social life are a blend. Priming day is a social event as well as a workday. The men are in the field about seven in the morning picking the mature tobacco leaves from the bottom of the plant. They work with a mule-drawn slides, or narrow carts with runners instead of wheels, which move through the rows of tobacco. When a primer gets an armload of leaves, he puts them in the slide and moves on. The mule is an animal especially suited for this work because he is slow and more patient than a horse and more able to sustain the summer heat. He can stand still for long periods and then, on command, move only a few steps to the next position. Tobacco has a sticky yellow gum which turns green or brownish green on the hands. It is difficult to scrub off. Many a tobacco farmer has permanently green brown or yellow hands.

The women and children gather at the barn about nine o'clock to tie the tobacco on sticks, and prepare it to be put up in the barn for curing. Tobacco was tied in bunches of three or four leaves on a stick about two feet long. The men later fill the barn with tied tobacco and then spend three days and nights firing the barn through flues, which send heat to cure the tobacco from its natural green color to a golden yellow. The better the curing process, the better the price at market. Rich golden leaves bring the best price.

Putty was the first person to take me into and up to the top of a tobacco barn. We climbed, log over log, one at a time until we reached the top. We sat there and breathed in the sweetness of cured tobacco. Although the barn was empty, the odor of cured tobacco filled every inch of my nostrils. I have never been an enthusiast of burning tobacco in a lit cigarette but unlit cured tobacco hanging in a barn is an aphrodisiac. Some days, if we could lose Jake, we climbed into the barn to read *Tropic of Cancer*.

One or two women tie-*ers* tie the tobacco on sticks. The other women and children put together bunches of leaves and handed them to the tie-*ers*. There is not much to think about while doing this so there is time for socializing and gossiping. A circle of belonging is created. I worked with them and I played with them. I was with them for many summers. I belonged.

The summer was not all work. On very hot days, Sara took all the farm kids to the river for a swim. She hated to drive so any one of us tall enough to reach the pedals and see over the steering wheel was allowed to drive the flivver. Remember, it was rural country. I started driving when I was about twelve. The first time I drove, I backed the car out of the garage, turned it around, lost control, and took off through a cornfield. I tore down stalks in ten rows before I was able to find the brake. My father was never pleased with my sallies into things he thought were dangerous. Had he been with us on the farm I would have been grounded for the rest of the summer. The incident would have ended my driving career. Sara however, was more tolerant and thought of the happening as just one more episode in my education.

After a rainfall, the river was muddy and inhabited by water snakes but it was wet and refreshing. There were large boulders in the middle of the river that created a waterfall when the water rushed downstream. We climbed the boulders and jumped into the rushing waters or swam under the waterfall to hide from each other. We tried to catch the river trout with our hands but they were too fast for us. The snakes were the worst. They congregated in the shallow water along the banks of the river. If I waded into the river without seeing a snake, I was all right to swim because few snakes came into deeper water. If by chance, a water moccasin brushed past my foot as I entered the river that was the end of my swim. I was terrified. For the farm kids I was the object of much teasing. While I hustled back to shore, they set about catching snakes to make pets of them.

The mahogany red North Carolina clay soil washed into the river and permeated the river so that it ran red, coloring everything it touched. Skin, hair, and bathing suit required the attention of the washboard when we got home. I enjoyed life as a temporary red head, a joy I approximate every six or seven weeks in my present life.

Better than a trip to the river was a trip to the pool. If Sara had to go into town on business or do some shopping, she dropped us off at the pool and picked us up after she completed her chores. Pools are better than rivers - no snakes and no red mud. Southern towns were different from northern towns. In the south, you saw signs, which said, "No Colored," "Whites only." The terms Afro-American or Blacks were not in use then. People were referred to as *Colored* or *Nigras,* the southern pronunciation of the word Negro. Of course, the "N" word was also used. No one thought of this as derogatory. There was little sensitivity to the feelings of the Afro American community.

There were never black people at the pool. There were separate public bathrooms and drinking fountains for black people and white people. Schools and churches were also segregated. If a white person and a black person approached each other on the street, the Black person stepped off the sidewalk and let the white person pass. Usually the Black person nodded or tipped a hat to the white person as a sign of

100

respect. It was here that I learned that the word *BLUE* in the name of a restaurant or motel was the code for a facility for Afro- Americans. I learned first hand about the Jim Crow Laws, which sought to prevent blacks from exercising their civil rights. If you traveled by train from any part of the South going north, the last car was for colored people. When you got to Washington, you changed trains and lost the "Colored Only" car.

There was a strange relationship between the races. The whites genuinely believed that the black people were an inferior race. They believed they were children who had to be disciplined and cared for. If not kept in their place, blacks would be destructive to themselves and to the rest of society. Remnants of the plantation system survived in the notion of Black people that they were to be cared for and the notion of the whites that they will care for the Blacks as long as everyone plays by the white man's rules. It worked for them until Rosa Parks decided not to move to the back of the bus. As a child, I accepted this naive concept; as an adult, I cannot believe the incredible ignorance involved. What you are told as a child, you believe. How easy it is to persuade children. For the most part, I saw blacks being treated well. I was not perceptive enough to realize the subtle indignity of the situation.

101

Thomas Merton tells the story of writing to a Jewish friend who resettled from New York to Alabama. He suggested his friend blacken his face so he would be all three things the Southerners disliked most –Yankees, Jews, and Blacks. That was not my experience. I was a New Yorker and a Catholic, two of the things of which the Southerners of Stokes Pines had little knowledge. I was a curiosity to them. There were endless questions about New York City and the New York Yankees baseball team. It was my fifteen minutes of fame. My talent for Irish hyperbole crested during tobacco curing evenings down at the barn. Throw another marshmallow on the fire and yarn another tale about the golden streets of New York. Tell of the glamorous men and women you spotted walking on Fifth Avenue or darting into a taxicab.

I remember the first time I realized that women were discriminated against in society and in the workplace. I watched women of the nineteen hundred seventies burn bras, march in

protest and wondered what they had to complain about. Life was good. Women were free and had the vote, we worked alongside men, we attended college, we enjoyed the amenities of life. What I did not see was the trivialization of women's lives in much the same way the lives of Black people were considered insignificant. As I began to understand the Black people of the United States who rose up to protested against discrimination I saw the subtleties of their plight and finally saw that women were in a similar if less intense situation.

In Stokes Pines, good Blacks were treated well though never treated as equals, and bad Blacks were treated harshly. There was Aunt Mary, a good Methodist woman. Good Black women were always called Aunt something and good Black men were called Uncle something. There was no Black Church within walking distance for Aunt Mary in Stokes Pines. She was a Bible reading, prayerful woman who felt the need to pray in a community. She cleaned, did laundry, and cooked for Sara as well as for other women in the community. She baked the best biscuits in the county. Waking up to the aroma of hot biscuits permeating the house on a sunny July morning was enough to charm my nutritional over-achiever body out of bed hours before it was prepared to meet the day.

Aunt Mary took it into her head that she wanted to go to church, sing hymns and pray with other folks. The first Sunday she showed up at church and sat in the last row, tongues did more than pray. She was there the next Sunday and the next Sunday and all the Sundays thereafter. She

103

was a woman of great dignity and presence. No one had the gumption to challenge her. The Methodist church in Stokes Pines was integrated.

Going to church was special. It was the one-day in the week in summer that people wore shoes. Not everyone had shoes so, if you were without, you did not attend services in the winter, but shoeless in summer was acceptable. It strikes me as amazing that in a situation where all people in the community are afflicted with equal amounts of poverty, human nature will still find a way to make distinctions even if only distinctions in levels of poverty. "My poverty is one step above ours so I am better than you." Most people went barefoot from April to November. I remember feeling inferior because my tenderfoot feet were unable to cope unshod. My attempts to show off ended in walking on my ankles for they were less velvety than the soles of my feet. However, when rain soaked the red North Carolina clay soil, it was glorious to have your bare feet in the soft fleshy mud. There was exhilaration of being unbound and at one with the earth.

The girls wore Sunday Go to Meeting Dresses their mothers sewed from flour sacks or animal feed sacks. Many of these sacks had colorful flower prints on them. It was often the case where two or three girls showed up wearing a dress made from the same flour sack material. The only difference was the creativity of a mother to change the dress pattern by adding a sash or a different collar. No one seemed to mind the similarities. The boys wore their Sunday overalls and a shirt made from a flour sack.

Church started at nine o'clock and lasted until noon. We sang hymns, listened to the preacher read a passage from the Bible and make comments about it. The children were divided by age group and sent to various parts of the church with their Sunday School Teachers for further instruction. We learned the parables as children's stories. I could never figure out why Jonah was in that whale or why God wanted Abraham to kill his son. Wasn't murder wrong? Religion was strange!

The preacher frightened me. Often he told of the horrors of hell. The fires of damnation would burn your soul for all eternity! I wasn't sure what a soul was and eternity seemed like a very long time. I once burned my finger trying to light a candle. The pain stayed with me for two days. I was not about to mess with going to hell. Sometimes he mentioned one of the young people in the community who was doing too much drinking, smoking, engaging in shameless sex, and card playing who was on his way to damnation.

We prayed for Amos, the sixteen-year-old son of Thalmal and Sarah Carlson, and hoped he would mend his ways and come to church. When Amos was killed in an auto accident while drunk, I was frightened. I was convinced his soul was suffering in hell at that very moment. Amos often drove us to the pool or the river in Sara's pickup truck on days when she was too busy to take us. Putty, Jake, Mille, and I loved to ride standing up in the back of the truck, hair, and clothing swept behind us as the wind rushed passed. Putty's long putty colored hair managed to get in everyone's mouth as we bounced, at fifty miles an hour, along the pothole littered dirt road. Amos was intent on sending one or another of us ricocheting out of the truck and on to the road. We knew the game and hung on like winter does before the stirring of a late spring. Down at the river we smoked Camel cigarettes, or rolled our own from the tobacco we appropriated from the barn the previous evening, and we swam. The exhilaration of the forbidden clung to me like shame clings to the sinner. It was more fun to go to the river with Amos than with Sara. I cried for Amos and worried about his soul.

Religion was simple and to the point. You work hard, you pray hard, you do good and at the end you can expect to go to heaven. There was little theology beyond that. They did not ponder the world's great theological or philosophical questions. They accepted quite literally the words and teaching of the King James Bible. Jonah was down in that whale arguing with God to let him out; Noah made sure he had two of all living things. I often wished Noah had made an exception when it came to snakes.

As I have mentioned, Stokes Pines was in a dry county of North Carolina. Yet, the mountains were littered with stills producing illegal moonshine. If you walked ten minutes into any direction in the back woods, you found a still. No one would admit to taking a drink. No one, except Sara, would offer a drink to another. Her childhood friend Wallace dropped in most afternoons just before dinnertime and then again evenings after eight o'clock to share a few swig of the good stuff. His blue Ford pickup truck was the cue to the neighborhood that it was drinking time at Raddy's. Miss Tess, Wallace's tee totaling wife was humiliated that her husband spent more time with Sara than he spent with her. She was embarrassed that he managed to stay drunk most nights and that he was not a Church going man. I should have been more sympathetic of Miss Tess but I did not like her much and Wallace was my friend.

Wallace and Sara knew each other from early childhood and were good friend. He was in love with her since fifth grade. Had she not gone to New York they would have married. Miss Tess imagined the orgies going on at the big house and wanted her husband home. She should not have worried. Sara was in love with someone else.

Of all the dull people I have met in my life, Miss Tess is one of the dullest. Her conversation was limited to back fence gossip. Chief among her targets was the loose living hell bound Sara. At least Daisy talked to her cow. To me, Wallace was a hero. He told gossipy stories about folks but coming from his mouth, the stories were not malicious for he saw the humor and the absurdity in the human condition. He knew his own weakness and was tolerant of the weakness of others.

He let me drive his pick-up truck; he sided with me when Hilary complained about me to her mother. Drinking was a serious sin. I worried about Sara going to heaven. Nevertheless, there was little to do except party in Stokes Pines. When white youths drank, they were sowing their oats. When Black youths drank, they suffered a stiffer condemnation. In bed on weekend nights, I heard the hooting of teenagers drunk on moonshine tearing up the dirt roads in their pickup trucks and shooting off their rifles enjoying the merriment of their youth. I longed to be a teenager. It had to be so much fun. Sunday morning gossip at church started with, "Did y'all hear 'em young ones last night? They like to kill 'emselves speeding across the holler. The drink will kill all of 'em."

One Saturday night the preacher's boy Josh, was arrested for drunk driving. A few weeks earlier, he and Lula Jane, his true love, were discovered naked in her daddy's barn. The twin boys she later gave birth to had the exact shade of crimson curly hair as Josh. The scandal was so bad the preacher was asked to leave and a replacement arrived about six weeks later. He had no children so he was safe from rowdy teenagers drinking and having sex in the back of pickup trucks.

The second deadly sin in this tobacco country was smoking. However, here was more discrimination. The smoking ban was only for women, the other minority group. Men rolled their own cigarettes, smoked pipes and cigars, snuffed and chewed tobacco, but women were considered fallen angels if they smoked. Naturally, the women went underground. An unexpected visitor could be kept waiting at the door for ten minutes while the lady of the house tried to clear the cigarette smoke from the kitchen. Miss Tess was a chain smoker. She swore the smell of tobacco on her clothing was the result of Wallace smoking in the house. Wallace knew better but he never said anything. I guess the way to make an activity flourish is to ban it.

Cousin Nanny Lee Clark was kin to Sara, as was almost everyone else in Stokes Pines. If ten people were standing together, nine were probably related. The tenth was a tourist or someone like me. About 1753, the people of Stokes Pines followed the Wagon Trail down from Philadelphia, Delaware and Maryland. They were told to go south where land could be bought for about fifteen cents an acre. Often a squatter could stake out a claim at no cost. They were mostly Moravians, Scots, Germans, Irish, and some French. By wagon, they came down an old Indian path that today is known as the Cumberland Trail. A 1750's map indicates the distance was about four hundred thirty-five miles. They settled into the mountains, married, inter-married, and didn't reconnect with the modern world until well after the Second World War. There is an old joke in the North that says if two Southerners get married and then divorced, are they still cousins?

Cousin Nanny Lee Clark was the oldest person I had ever seen. It was Sara's custom to visit Cousin Nanny Lee Clark whenever we passed her cousin's home on the way to or from town. She was never addressed as Nanny Lee, or Mrs. Clark but always as Cousin Nanny Lee

Clark. As often as we visited, I never saw Cousin Nanny Lee Clark out of bed. She sat propped up in bed fully clothed in a long white cotton dress with frilly ruffles down the front. Her elongated neck was completely covered with white ruffles. Long sleeves extended to just below her wrist. It was always the same white dress. Perhaps she had several like it. She wore heavy white stockings, a wig, and the traditional country farm bonnet made from a flower sack.

Her hands fascinated me. They were as large and as white as any I have ever seen on a Halloween skeleton. They were long, bony, and like porcelain. She spoke in a whisper audible only if you leaned over and put your ear to her mouth. She often pulled me over close to her to whisper something in my ear. I was so frightened I could not hear what she said. Most of the time, I thought I was looking at a dead woman. The room was as dark as any room could be in the middle of summer. The heavy curtains were always drawn, as Cousin Nannie Lee Clark could not tolerate light. A pitcher of water was always on the nightstand next to her bed. She and Sara often shared a glass of water but Hilary and I were never offered a cool drink of water. We were sent to the kitchen for a glass of milk. I am not sure they were drinking water. They talked about the good old days when Sara's father, Mr. Tom was a wealthy tobacco manufacturer and of

111

the days when the young were more respectful. I was insecure and guilt ridden enough to think they were talking about me. Sara agreed there was too much drinking, smoking, and sex these days. I was certain she knew about my days at the river with Amos.

I never quite figured out how Sara and Cousin Nanny Lee Clark were related. I suspect they were not cousins at all but Sara was the niece and Cousin Nanny Lee Clark was Mr. Tom's older sister. Perhaps she was sensitive about her age. To be a cousin sounded younger than an aunt.

One day Cousin Nanny Lee Clark did die. Her daughter, Easter, born on an Easter Sunday morning, sent for Sara to come help prepare Cousin Nanny Lee Clark for burial. It was the custom for the women of the family and neighbors to prepare the body for burial. I was chosen to come along. More education!

We went into the kitchen where Cousin Nanny Lee Clark was laid out on the long oak table. I had often been treated to milk and homemade cookies at the same table. She was completely covered with the white sheet that had been a permanent part of her bed. Her face and neck were visible. I realized she was not wearing her white dress. She no longer wore her wig. I could see that she was quite bald. There was a quarter on each of her eyelids. There were two basins of hot water one on either side of the table. Easter was there along with three neighbor women. When Sara arrived, the sheet was drawn back and the women began to wash the body. Cousin Nanny Lee Clark had two of the largest, longest breasts I have ever seen before or since. Easter tossed each breast over her mother's shoulder to allow the women to wash the skin underneath them. They landed with a thud on the wooden table behind her head. I was uncomfortable but more concerned about the new growth I observed in myself.

I had two pasties beginning to sprout on my chest. They were barely the size of two small pimples. They amounted to a scarcely perceptible slight rise on my contour. For two weeks, I had nightmares in which I saw myself with breasts which hung down below my knees and which could be slung over my shoulder and tied in a knot behind my head. If I bent over, they swept the ground and swayed from side to side causing me to lose my balance. I dreamed I would not go to school for fear my appendages would be first and second base at recess. During the day, I pressed my hands hard against my chest so the little things would not grow. I wore tight band-aids to stunt their development. Nothing helped.

They grew and grew. Would I soon look like Cousin Nanny lee Clark?

Sara soaked a cloth in camphor and placed it over her cousin's face. She said it was so the face would not lose color. However, she looked purple to me. Sara placed a slice of cucumber under each quarter. She pried open her cousin's mouth and removed the false teeth. These she placed in a glass with baking soda and water. She handed the glass to Easter and suggested that when the time came, Easter might be happy to have her mother's teeth as her own.

As they worked, they chatted about how wonderful a woman Cousin Nanny Lee Clark had been. She was a God-fearing, church-going woman who never did anyone any wrong. She had just celebrated her one-hundredth birthday, outliving her husband Jeb by forty-two years. Although she had eight pregnancies, Easter was the only one to survive to adulthood. Five babies were still born and two died in infancy. She did not curse God but accepted all as her lot. She worked beside Jeb in the tobacco fields all their married life. When he died, she buried him on the farm down in the holler beside his mother and father and alongside his grandparents, great grandparents, and great great grandparents. Five generations were tobacco farmers and good church going Methodists. Now the farm would

114

pass to Easter, her husband, and the generations to follow them. The yellow stains from tobacco gum, made their hands a permanent yellow, and were, after so many generations, a genetic part of their make up.

When they finished, they wrapped her in a black shroud and placed her in the coffin that the men carried in from the barn. The coffin, manufactured by Easter's husband was made from wood slabs that were once part of the old barn. The new barn, built just a year ago, was constructed from the two eighty five year old pine tress at the edge of the north field. One had been struck by lightning and felled. The other had outgrown its space so that its roots were growing under and ruining the tobacco plants.

That night the women took turns sitting up with the body laid out in the parlor. Easter remained awake all night and tended to the food and drink needs of her sister mourners. She made three batches of biscuits and served them with blue berry jam made from the blue berries she picked and canned last fall. She served hot coffee laced with moonshine. About three o'clock in the morning the ladies became ebullient and the chatter and giggles turned to stories of their husbands as lovers. There was talk of which husbands slept with women in the community other than their wives. Of course, husbands of the women present were the quintessence of marital fidelity. They were careful not to tread on each other's sensitivities. By morning, no one remembered the conversations of the previous night. A blessing!

The next morning the preacher came along with most folks from the community. We sang the hymns, *I'm Comin' Over Lord,* and *Rock of Ages.* Two of Cousin Nanny Lee Clark's kinfolk passed out and had to be revived with smelling salts. Other women fell on the floor in grief. The women wailed and the men spit chewing tobacco. The preacher talked about the fires of hell and how sure he was that Cousin Nanny Lee Clark, good woman that she was, was enjoying heaven. He passed the hat. Some people deposited chicken eggs. Some left a sack of flour. I had a nickel, which I dropped into the hat.

After the service, the men carried her body down to the hollow near the spring and buried her in the grave Easter's husband dug the day before. It was customary for each family to fence in a portion of their land as the family burial plot. Farms stayed in the same family generation after generation. Today, as farms are broken up into three or four-acre building lots, the cemeteries survive with an easement that allows access to the plot for future burials. Most of the original families are still living in and around Stokes Pines and continue to bury family members in the family plots.

Everyone brought food, which was spread out on the table where Cousin Nanny Lee Clark had lain. There was fried chicken, biscuits, corn on the cob, tomatoes, corn bread, and snap beans. The men stealthily tiptoed out back by the barn for moonshine and men talk. They worried about the weather affecting their crops and about the price tobacco would bring at auction in the fall.

Life was hard so to die at the age of one hundred was a mixed blessing. Most people, and women in particular, hoped to die many years before the century mark. Their simple faith taught that life in heaven would be better than the hardships of farm life in Stokes Pines. Tobacco farming is backbreaking work, which can come to nil if there is even a small glitch in the weather. Raising a gaggle of children who must pass their shoes down to the next one or who do not have enough clothing to get through the winter is a constant worry. Women get old early.

Ten

The train out of Grand Central to Westchester was on the Saturday schedule yet running late as usual. The jeans and tee shirt crowd returning from a matinee or a day of shopping in the city did not seem to mind the delay. There was an atmosphere of leisure and early spring breakout after a frigid winter that held them imprisoned by the northeast's most brutal four months in fifty years.

Leonard settled into reading the *New York Times* and felt again like a commuter returning home after work. He was anxious to see his children but not looking forward to another encounter with Whitney. He was sorry he agreed to take her to the annual kick-off -the-season dinner dance at the country club. Maura was out of town. He was feeling sorry for himself and lonely when Whitney called. She well knew he was not a match for her or for any woman's tears. She argued she could not face their friends and do all the explaining by herself. This separation and divorce was not her idea nor was she going to try to explain his recent idiotic career move. She had her pride and position in the community to maintain. She would not be made a fool of in front of her friends.

As the train huffed to a halt in the station, Leonard caught sight of Whitney, Lenny, Abby, and Jodie searching each window eager to be the first to catch a glimpse of him. Abby was the first to see him and squealed with excitement. As he stepped down from the last step of the train, the two girls were there to smother him with hugs and kisses. Lenny hung back beside his mother. He had grown another three inches and towered over her. Leonard could not determine if he was being the man of the house for his mother or if he was exhibiting the natural reticence of a young boy coming into puberty uncomfortable with a show of affection to another male. Whitney greeted him with a kiss on the cheek and a cool handshake. It was an awkward drive to the house with Whitney driving instead of him. He was never comfortable in a car with someone else driving, much less his wife. The car was his

119

domain. Weekday mornings she drove with him to the train station then she drove the car home. Other than shopping, doing daily chores and ferrying the children to their various activities, she was not behind the wheel. Lenny was a basketball player and the girls were on the swim team. She did not enjoy driving but much preferred the comfort of being catered to. Now she showed him who is in charge. The two girls chatted on, their words stepping on each other as they related all that had occurred since he last saw them. Lenny remained quiet except for an occasional correction to the narrations of his sisters.

Once inside the house Whitney hustled everyone off to assignments. Abby grabbed Leonard's overnight bag ran up stairs and put it in the master bedroom. Lenny got Schnitzel's leach and took the German Shepard for a long overdue walk. Jodie trailed around behind her father, talked incessantly as he inspected the lawn and the contents of the garage. It would soon be time to start mowing. Whitney called to him, "We must hurry, or we'll be late for the cocktail hour. I had your tuxedo cleaned and pressed. It is hanging on the door of your closet. Please get dressed."

Except for Lenny, everyone was treating him as though he had merely been away on the usual business trip and was now home. Life was as it always was. Neither Whitney nor the children were dealing with the reality. Daddy is here just for the weekend; to help Mommy get through the difficult first weekend of the new social season and of course, to spend some time with his son and two daughters. He missed them. Leonard told himself he could not go back to the life that suffocated him for so many years. His children would have to understand and in time, they would.

Mildred Sweeney and her garden committee worked for days to transform the Club's main dining room into an Hawaiian paradise of tropical flora. The theme for this year is Island Paradises Around The World. Hawaii was the first to be followed next month by Pago Pago, She and her husband Martin spent ten days in Hawaii and returned home insistent everyone go native. Marty's tuxedo shirt was not the usual white but a multicolored floral number he picked up while on the island. The conventional black bow tie and black cummerbund were all he had left of his dignity. After the fourth and last of their brood graduated from college, Marty retired from the banking business. They decided not to spend their days in the empty nest but to go on perpetual vacations and keep in touch with the family and friends via post cards from around the world. It was apparent Marty had started the evening earlier than seven o'clock. He was at least three-drinks-up on everyone else. Mildred, who usually keeps track of her husband, was too busy moving potted palms to notice.

Marty spotted Leonard across the room and surreptitiously moved toward him. "Leonard, old boy, we've missed you." He pulled Leonard toward him; leaned into his ear and said, "Hear you got yourself a live young one in the City. Wish I had the guts to do that." His words bit through the jangle of glasses and assorted small talk, "Hope my wife doesn't catch me talking to you. She says you are a son-of-a-bitch."

It was not the time nor the place to take on a drunk, instead Leonard extracted himself and beat his way through palm trees and hibiscus to the bar to get a scotch and water for himself and a white wine for Whitney. George Atwater and Harold Weiner were at the bar also getting drinks for themselves and for their wives. Each gave Leonard a cordial nod and a polite, "Good to see you," then moved on to deliver drinks and conversation with others in the room. George, and Harold along with Jim McDougal were Leonard's Saturday morning golf foursome. Over the years, they became good golf, poker, and drinking friends. Their wives were like sisters.

As Leonard headed back to Whitney, he saw that her sister wives had gathered around like worker bees protecting the queen. The news that the despicable "other woman" at the office victimized her and her children spread in sheets of sound over the air waves. They assured her of their support for her and the children. After all she sacrificed for Leonard and the children she deserved better than this. He has three beautiful children a beautiful and doting wife and a lovely home. What is the matter with men? Not the best of them can be trusted. Women must stick together. Each guaranteed to be there for her.

Leonard felt as though he were swimming in a pond of alligators. He handed Whitney her wine then tried to escape to a more friendly shore among the men. George and Harold, while polite were not their usual jovial back slapping selves. He saw Jim McDougal heading for the men's room and followed him in.

"I see the local madams of righteousness have taken my wife under their wings. They make me feel as dirty as subway graffiti. " he told Jim as the two stood side by side at the urinal.

"Sorry about that Len. Most of the guys understand. You would not have done it if you did not have to. One time or another we have all been in that spot. Two years ago, I had a fling at the office. It was great but not good enough to throw away my marriage and home." Jim did not

123

understand that it wasn't about his marriage. It was about his life. He loved his kids and his wife but the life style was choking him.

"You are a married woman's worst nightmare. You threaten the entire structure of her life. From her point of view, if you get away with this then every wife in the community is not safe from similar behavior from her husband. Have you noticed the icy air around you?"

"There are two sides to every story. Isn't anyone interested in my side?"

"Buddy, in this situation there is only one side ... hers! The guys will talk to you privately but not within light years of their wives. This is war. You are the enemy and you are to be taught a lesson."

"You guys afraid of your wives?"

"You bet! Lots of guys would like to do what you did but the cost is too high. So, we keep things in check and do a bit of playing around on the side. No big deal."

Leonard went back to the party, made small talk for the rest of the evening, and pretended he did not notice the frigid reception he received from his former friends. He downed five more scotches then barely made it to the car. Whitney had to drive home. He vaguely remembered her raging about his barbaric behavior in front of her friends.

A crack of Sunday morning light escaped around the drawn window shade of the master bedroom. With great effort, Leonard managed to open one eye toward the digital clock on the night table. He saw that it was after one pm. He put one foot on the floor and then the other. His head pounded and he was feeling nauseous. As he raised his body out of bed, he realized he was wearing pajamas. He had not worn pajamas since he left Westchester. He hated peejays but his wife insisted it was crude to sleep without them. It was then he became conscious of where he was. He had planned to sleep in the guest room. He wondered if he slept with Whitney.

He found his old toothbrush and electric shaver in the medicine cabinet. There was a surreal quality about the day. It was as though he had never been away. As he shaved, he put together the pieces from last evening. Whitney had set him up. This was his punishment. He abandoned her. He was to see what it felt like to have everyone walk away. As he dressed, anger smoldered through his entire body. He wanted to tear her apart for this vicious premeditated plan.

125

The house seemed very quiet. Schnitzel followed him into the bathroom and tagged along behind with every move he made, as he got dressed. When he got downstairs he found a note on the kitchen table. "Took the girls to their swim meet. Len has a basketball game. You know where everything is. Have breakfast. Talk to you later." He was too hung over to think about eating. He called a taxi and took the three o'clock train back to the City.

Eleven

My new stepfamily turned out to be unwelcoming. They were not aware of my existence and looked on me as an intruder into the sorrow of their family. The three daughters were especially protective of their mother and hostile to my presence at Dad's wake and funeral. However, there was no way I was going away and let my father be put to his final rest without being part of it. Leonard felt I should leave since it appeared that neither my father nor any of his new family was happy with my being there.

Marty Flynn was my only ally. He was the only person who knew I existed and he was sworn to secrecy. For many years Dad presented himself as an unattached bachelor. He had not been in touch with Alice or Jack for eons. He guessed that Alice was dead since he had not heard from her in several years. He was not interested in hearing from Jack after so many years of alienation from him. It is not true that time heals wounds. Wounds deepen and alienation sets in with time. With time, imagination magnifies wounds. Dad was bitter because of the many years he had to pay alimony and child support. For him when the marriage was over he wanted it put behind him. The weekly payments were a constant and bitter reminder that he was tethered to a wife and son for whom he no longer cared.

"Your father was getting older and needed someone to take care of him. Rosie cared for him as though he were her child. She bought him clothes; she cooked for him; she catered to his every wish; she mothered him. They were living together and your father felt it only right to make an honest woman of her"

I recalled my Aunt Mary saying Dad never got over the death of his mother. Until today I did not really know what she meant. His mother babied him every day of her life and well into his manhood. No other woman could measure up. In relationships with women he sought out mother–son rather than husband wife alliances. For the first time I understood a part of my father's personality which was a mystery to me. In his declining days he regained his mother. There are traumas in life we do not survive. We may pass through them and move on to other things but what has truly affected us remains. It colors everything that life sends our way. It becomes our life mystery. It is the reason for everything we do. It is central to who we are. Is there one thread, which dominates a life; which is weaved through every seemly random decision we make? What is my life mystery, I wondered? Is it the trauma of loss and being rootless which runs around my life in a vague sort of way that is the motivator for my life? Was the fear of loss the reason I found commitment so difficult? I never put it together but will spend time looking into this new idea. Suddenly I had a new respect and a new understanding of my father. I felt ashamed for condemning him for not making a better life for him and for me. Was I any better?

By the second day of dad's wake, not only was I not welcome in the stepfamily but also I was making myself obnoxious by asking Marty dozens of question he could not or would not answer. Rosie and her three daughters not only ignored me but also made nasty remarks about why I had to be here. It was their impression that since Dad never mentioned me, I had abandoned him. There was no point in trying to explain that that was Dad's modus operandi. He would disappear from my life for months at a time without explanation or presumably without any reason. I seldom knew where he was or what he was doing. I never understood this need for secrecy and privacy in his life. Sometimes when he surface I discovered he had spent several months in Florida fishing. Other times he just moved to another neighborhood in the city. One day he would call and say, "Hi, what's doing?" and continue a conversation as though we talked only yesterday. I lost him many times over. I was accustomed to having him disappear but this time was different. He was never coming back. For months after the funeral I waited for his call. Every time the phone rang I anticipated hearing his voice saying, "Hi."

I could not get Alice and Jack out of my mind. If there were two widows there could be legal as well as fiscal problems. There were benefits to be paid to the widow from Social Security and from Dad's printers' union as well as an insurance policy or two. After the funeral I needed to locate Jack and get the lay of the land.

It was almost a relief when on the third day we boarded the limousines, went to the church and then to the cemetery. There is little in life, which is harder than to watch as your parent is lowered into the grave. There is such finality. All the guilt of a lifetime cruises in. Why wasn't I a better daughter? I needed to say good-bye but there was no time. I wanted just one more moment. Perhaps the hurts of a lifetime could have been healed.

I threw a rose into the grave, turned and went back to the car. That night I clung to Leonard. He held me as I cried, mourned my father and felt very sorrow for myself. I wondered what death is. Each loss is a death. We are dying all the time. We should be prepared for the final loss but we are not. What had my father's life meant? What does any life mean? Here I am at Sara's deathbed. What does her life mean?

Twelve

I watched Sara labor to breath with the aid of the oxygen mask she had attached to her faced. I remembered the many down home folk remedies she taught me and realized how they were of no help to her now. She shared with me her country folk view of life. Life was hard and real and unsentimental.

Today's health conscious population ingest ginseng to keep themselves healthy. The people of Stokes Pines knew the benefits of ginseng long before moderns became aware of the marvels of herbs and roots. This perennial plant grows in the shelter of their thick woods, along the creeks and knolls in the area. People believed it to be a cure for everything from the common cold to cancer. It was either chewed or made into a tonic - which prolonged life and kept the system healthy - by placing it into a bottle of moonshine. So, those who did not drink had their tonic to get them through the night.

Country people thrive on superstitions and homespun sayings. My Stokes Pine friends were no different. It was a way of educating the young and keeping adults in line with local customs and mores. Daisy and Miss Tess were often quoted as punctuating situations with one or more of their favorite Stokes Pine-isms "Kill a granddaddy spider and your cow will go dry." Was Daisy's reason for allowing the cobwebs to gather in the corner of the kitchen. "If you work on Easter Monday you will lose the worth of a cow. If by chance, you do not get to work any day during the week, never start on Friday." Wallace was fond of telling Tess all work and no moonshine made him a dull husband. "It is bad luck to twirl a chair. To break the bad luck, stand it up, spit in it, and twirl it backwards three times." Wallace came to my rescue the day I broke the milking stool in the barn. "If a baby doesn't fall off the bed by itself, it will never live to get grown." I do not remember where I heard this but it has stuck in my brain for many years.

Daisy told me many times, "A north branch makes the best likker."

"It's not a disgrace to get the itch: but it is to keep it." This is a personal favorite of Sara. I heard her say it repeatedly to the many visitors to the manor. When Sara heard gossip about her from one of the neighbor's she shrugged it off with, "Don't spit in the well; you may have to drink the water." For Hilary and me she kept us on the straight and narrow with, "The devil has many tools, but a lie is the handle which fits all of them."

Back in New York, I entertained my friends and my fathers' friends by repeating the sayings in my best southern drawl. These customs, and sayings are not known in New York. New York saying were more in the genre of P.T. Barnum who said, "Never educate a drunk and never give a sucker an even break." The cynicism of New Yorkers is legendary.

There was no sentimentality toward animals. These mountain people were very secure in their understanding that humans are humans and animals are animals. People have souls and are going to heaven; animals do not have souls and are going no place. There was no coddling of dogs, cats or any pet. Each pet had a purpose and there was no fooling about that. Cats rid the farm of rats and mice and dogs hunt with you and are guardians of the chicken coop. They lived outside year round and ate table scraps. Alpo would have been laughed at. The common belief was that dogs with long tails were subject to a life of worms. Dogs' tails were cut down to a stump. A neighbor's dog delivered a litter of mutts and gave one to Sara. The poor animal developed a tail almost as long as its body. Surgery was coming.

It was my job to hold the dog's body while her friend Wallace held the tail, and Sara severed the tail with an axe. It was only a pup of seven months yet it had the strength of a fully mature dog. It struggled in my arms for I sensed it knew what was coming. I elected to hold this black and white longhaired mongrel in my arms rather than hold the end where Wallace was stationed because I did not want to be left with a bleeding unattached tail in my hand.

Sara quickly dipped the bleeding stump into kerosene and wrapped a tight gauze bandage on it. The howling animal took off, crawled under the woodpile, and remained there for three days after which it came out still wearing the blood caked bandage. I could never look that animal in the eye again. I took every opportunity to make friends by sneaking treats to him but he wasn't interested.

The only dog to escape surgery was Maydor. He was a retired great dane show dog who was brought down south to spend his declining days on the farm. He belonged to one of Sara's New York businessmen friends, Sam Holtzman. Maydor weighed more than two hundred pounds, had a head the size of a ten-inch television set, and jowls, which slobbered saliva when he shook his head. He was fierce to look at because of his size and the size of his head and teeth. His growl and bark were deep and menacing. He was a great watchdog. Strangers would not approach the house once they saw this giant. However, he was a gentle phony incapable of hurting even the fleas that aggravated him all summer. Maydor would have much preferred to summer in Maine than in North Carolina. He spent most of his time in the cool dirt under the back porch. He was

useless at a game of fetch. He made it very clear to all that he was retired and not about to play games or give pony rides. Unlike other dogs in the neighbor, Maydor was permitted to sleep in the house at night. It was thought he had arthritis, which meant the night air was harmful to his health. He curled up on the cool tile in front of the fireplace and snored most of the night. You felt safe at night if you heard Maydor snoring. No stranger would risk breaking into the house if he had to deal with the monster dog. The gossip of the farmers was that Maydor was a ridiculous canine specimen and not worth the two pounds of meat, he consumed in a day. His New York owner insisted on prime meat only. He was eating better than many of the farmers.

That same summer, the cow belonging to Sara's tenant farmer developed on its side, a boil the size of a grapefruit. The infection needed to be lanced and drained. If you could do it yourself, you never called the veterinarian. Sara, the farmer, and I got the cow on the ground on its side by tying her four legs together then pulling them out from under her. We tied the two front hoofs together and the two hind hoofs together. With a thunderous clunk, she fell over and let out a screeching, wailing moo. I held the back end, the milk end, and the farmer held the front end. He was able to grab her horns and twist her back to the ground if she tried to break free and get to her feet.

Sara sterilized a long butcher knife and lanced the boil. Puss erupted into the air then fell down all over the side of the cow. We had boiling water to wash away the infection and large bandages to tape over the wound. It was the first time I heard a cow cry. The wound needed to be cleaned out once a day for about a week. Each time it was necessary to turn that cow over on its side. Who needs a veterinarian? I think I threw up after both operations. If ever I entertained thoughts of becoming a vet, these experiences took the glamour out of the idea. I was, however, getting an education.

Sara was the kind of woman who would tackle anything that had to be done. She lived a full free life in which she made her own rules. She cared little for what anyone thought. Although she was not a favorite among the women adults in the community, the youngsters loved her, as did the men of Stokes Pines who thought of her as "A man's woman." She was good to all of the children. She took us swimming on hot days; she bought cold drinks and hotdogs; she made homemade ice cream; she sewed new clothes for us. We adored her. Hilary seldom joined in the fun. Sara saw me as more a daughter to her than Hilary was. We had more good times together than she had with Hilary. Maybe the other Hilary is right, "It takes a village to raise a child." Children often fare better and are happier with the parents of their friends than they are with their own parents. They are more able to talk to them and feel the other parent understand them better. I could talk to Sara when it was impossible to talk to my father.

While Sara and I were out saving the animal kingdom and ridding the world of chicken thieves, Hilary was at home moving furniture to make room for her dance rehearsal. Her passion was to be a ballerina. Short of that, she wanted to become a Rockette and dance at Radio City Music Hall in New York City. She pirouetted from the living room to the dining room to the kitchen and back to the living room. She used the railing on the front porch as an exercise bar. Day after day, the record player blared *The Nutcracker Suite* to all parts of the house. Tutu and toe-shoes were donned at the first sighting of any visitor to the house. She loved to perform and danced for hours or for as long as anyone could tolerate. I convinced myself she was only a so-so dancer. I knew I too could be a dancer as well as a celebrated brain surgeon. It only took my desire to do so and a little practice. However, my thrashings about on the living room floor were less nuanced by grace than by regiments of Spanish equestrians. The house shook and tables were knocked askew.

We were really quite different. I was spending my days mowing lawns, lancing boils on cows, cutting off dogs' tails, and playing nursemaid to chickens, she was blithely sashaying through the house in a tutu. In my next life, I want to come back as a Barbie Doll rather than as the Pumpkin Patch Kid that I am today.

Because of her, I took tap dancing lessons. Every Friday afternoon after school, we trotted over to Miss Julie's dance salon, donned our Mary Jane tap shoes, and sweated for an hour and a half. Hilary spent another hour and a half in toe shoes but I drew the line at ballet. I felt compelled to sit on the sideline and ridicule her and the other dancers. I was not popular at Miss Julie's. I learned the time step and participated in one dance recital before it was acknowledged that I was not meant for the stage. I was not meant to be a veterinarian, or horticulturist, either, so, my future was shaky.

Hilary's birthday was in late August. It tended to be the social event and the culminating event of the summer season. Preparation went on for days. The entire community was invited. A fiddle and banjo band was hired. An enormous cake was baked. It was always a white cake with Hilary's favorite, lemon icing frosting. Sara made homemade ice cream. Each of the young people took turns cranking the handle of the ice cream maker. The trick was to be the last person to turn the handle before Sara announced the ice cream was perfect for eating. As she removed the cover, the last handler was the first sampler of the ice cream located in the lid and the envy of all of us. Since the cake was made the day before the party, I usually licked the pan in which the birthday cake and icing were made. In the game of *one-up-man ship*, I was one up before the party began. Sara set up a bar out at the barn and away from the women. The men knew they were welcome to help themselves to the moonshine away from the watchful eyes of the womenfolk. Everyone pretended not to noticed the men making frequent trips to the barn or noticed the increasing joyfulness of the men folk. Wallace, usually a quiet observer, tittered sheepishly the entire afternoon.

Hilary prepared a new dance to perform. Sara created a costume for her for the dance and a red party dress for the party. She loved frilly taffeta dresses with layers of cloth. As she twirled, the dress spun away from her body. It was a dance in its own right – shiny, shimmery, luminous red, scattering like flames as she moved. She was primed to be the lady of the manor.

My friends, Millie, Putty, and Jake talked about the birthday party everyday from the first of July until the day it finally arrived. After the party, they talked about it all winter to their school friends. There was a scavenger hunt on the lawn, rides on old Molly and presents and prizes for everyone and of course the dance recital. People started arriving about noon and stayed until after dark. The music and the squeals of happy children rose into the Blue Ridge Mountains and echoed back. The party was fun, but I knew it meant we would soon be heading back to New York City. I never liked August

141

because it has been a symbol of endings for me. I do not deal well with endings or changes. They are signs of death, loss, and grief. The death of the summer, the loss, and grief of losing my friends for another year was more pain than I needed to tolerate. I cried when I had to leave Stokes Pines. I cried when I left New York City each year to spend the summer on the farm. It was a good life lesson for I learned early that life is a series of small deaths and losses until we come to the final death.

It is interesting that the people of Stokes Pines look at me with a certain amount of amazement because I was a Yankee and a New Yorker at that. They imagined New York as some exotic and frightening place filled with strange people and stranger life styles. They thought of New Yorkers as unfriendly, rude, and inhospitable. They wanted to go there to see the Yankees play baseball but, as the saying goes, would not want to live there. They did imagine that we lived an exciting life. Sara did all she could to foster this concept.

My life in Stokes Pines was much more exciting than my life in New York City. Life in New York was Automat, school, and playing in traffic. I envied the children of Stokes Pines and I suspect they envied me. They thought of their lives as dull and mine as exciting. How, in New

York, could I have had the experiences I had in Stokes Pines?

Before I arrived in Stokes Pines, the skeptic in me could not believe that mountains were anything but green. The Blue Ridge Mountains are blue. In the early morning and again at dusk they throw off a magical blue haze. At times, and up close, the enormous brooding southern pines blow tenderly across the night skyline, an apotheosis of Eden. Summers are warm but not oppressive with humidity as are New York summers. Many summer nights I stretched out on the lawn and looked straight up at the star filled sky. I traced the big dipper and the little dipper, and picked out a star that I claimed for myself, and name Maura. Warmth heals your soul as well as your flesh. I love those mountains.

At summers end, Sara sold flivver after flivver to farmers who promised to pay her in October when they sold their tobacco crop at auction and had money for a car and next year's seeds. We took the bus back north.

Thirteen

Sara decided that I was old enough at ten to know the real story of who I was. She sat me down at the kitchen table in her Washington Heights apartment. It was late in the evening just before I was to go to bed. The next day was a school day. I didn't know what was coming, but I knew it was not going to be good. I was convinced I was in trouble. What had I done that day? At least, what had I done that she knew about?

Alice's name was never spoken, nor was Jack's. It was an unwritten law, that neither I nor anyone else ever mentioned them. I still missed them and wondered if I would see them again. I still cried myself to sleep at night. Jack was a big boy by now. I imagined him as the smartest boy in his class. Would he attend as many schools as I? Dad did not appear to love him anymore. Would he no longer love me if I asked about Jack

144

and Alice? When Dad and Sara talked about Alice, they referred to her as FW - First Wife. "FW went into court today."" FW wants more alimony and child support."

Sara began, "You are old enough to know that Alice is not your real mother. Your mother died when you were born." She said it as gently as she could yet the words were out there. "Her name was Maura. You are named after her." "Alice is your step-mother." That was all there was to it. The subject was not mentioned again for many years. I asked no questions. I am not sure whether it was the trauma or a state of denial that prevented me from making further inquiry. Perhaps I didn't believe Sara, or perhaps I wanted things to be the way I had known them. I wanted Alice to be my mother. I wanted a real home with them. I wanted to stay in one place and go to the same school each year. I went to bed and cried myself to sleep. I felt disloyal to Alice and Jack because I did not defend them but the fear of more bad news overtook me. I was too much a coward to deal with more pain.

Finding a place where I belonged was more of a chore each year. I had no roots. I was alienated from Alice and Jack bouncing from place to place and from couch to couch with no fixed home. My family was my father and his come-a-day go-a-day friends. Sara and Hilary could not be counted on to be there because of the unstable relationship between Sara and Dad. Now I am told that my mother is not my mother. Some dead woman named Maura is my mother. No one knows anything about her or at least is unwilling to tell me about her. Dad will not say anything. I feel like an orphan adrift on my own undiscovered south Pacific island. The sense of being a small child alone in the world overwhelmed me. I began to obsess about my father's health and safety for if something happened to him, there would be no one to take care of me. I cried when he was not present especially at those times I was not sure where he might be. My concern was a selfish one for myself, spawned by my insecurity. I longed for aunts, uncles, cousins, and a family to call my own who would love and protect me.

There are photographs of me as a two-year-old child in the arms of my fraternal grandmother. I do not remember her. It never occurred to me that I lived with her for the first two years of my life. Of course, it must have been that way. Dad was a twenty-two year old widower with a new infant on his hands and no one to care for her. His only sibling was unmarried and living at home with their mother. I must have lived with them for a period of time.

When my grandmother died, Dad married Alice and we moved to Sunnyside, Long Island. There were stormy days. Mary, Dad's sister, despised Alice. I remember times when they roared at each other. One of my earliest memories is of Aunt Mary hurling a potted plant the length of the apartment hallway. It barely missed striking Alice.

The Phipps complex where we lived was composed of seven or eight apartment houses built around an interior courtyard. It was a child-friendly place where kids could ride bicycles, skate, and play in sand boxes. There was a clubhouse for adults. The men played cards and ping-pong. Dad played both endlessly. He also played with me. He taught me to ride a tricycle. He was a great fan of baseball so we played catch. In later years, he took me to see the Giants play at the Polo Grounds. As a Giant fan, he hated the evil Dodgers. He never forgave the team move to California. He lost his passion for baseball.

Alice's sister, Geneva, lived in another building in the complex with her son, Edmund, and her husband Ed. Ed and his father owned a bakery on Skillman Avenue. He was a harsh man who ruled not only his family with a cold Teutonic hand but ruled the extended family the same way. When Uncle Ed spoke, everyone paid attention and did as we were told. His wife,

Geneva, was a gentle soul who spoiled all the children in the family. She was my favorite. Edmund, and I loved playing in the bakery and stealing jelly donuts when Uncle Ed was not there. When Grandpa Ed was baking, he told us stories of his days as a young boy in Germany. The family had been bakers for five generations. We loved his charming German accent when he said, "apple strudel." We did everything to make him repeat the words then ran up to the front of the bakery giggling and mimicking him to the customers. We thought we were speaking German.

Alice and Geneva were young women when they came to New York from Boston. They were swimmers and had jobs in the water show at the New York Hippodrome. Geneva was a headliner who did a ten minute solo. They loved to tell stories about a fellow performer, Archibald Leach, who later became Cary Grant. Archie, a struggling actor like the others, was always hungry. Mrs. Farrell, Alice's and Geneva's mother, kept Archie in cookies baked with love in her south side of Boston kitchen.

Jack was born during the time we lived in the Phipps apartments. He was prone to colds that frequently progressed into pneumonia. Alice was a strong believer in the healing power of the sun and vitamin D. Mornings Jack was stripped down to only his diaper and set by the open kitchen window so the sunrays could reach his body. If a cloud blocked the sunlight, she quickly covered his naked body until the cloud passed. The outside temperature was often well below freezing. Jack was born in January and this therapy began soon after.

When the doctor decided a warmer climate was needed for Jack to survive, Alice, Jack, and I boarded a bus and headed for Daytona Beach, Florida. We rented a one-room apartment and remained there for the winter and several subsequent winters. Alice had a picture of Dad that once appeared in the *New York News* newspaper along with an answer he gave the newspaper's Inquiring Photographer. The reporter asked Dad what he would do if his house caught on fire. His response was that he would rush into the building and save his wife and two children. The piece was clipped from the paper, framed, and sat on the dresser in our small apartment. Each night as we said our prayers, Alice had us look at the clipping and picture, pray for Dad, tell him we love him and say goodnight. Whatever her differences were with him, she never let them affect our relationship with our father. We loved him dearly. Florida was warm and sunny. Tropical flowers blossomed everywhere you looked. We had tall red callas growing outside our window. It was always

149

summer. I missed winter sleigh riding but was more than happy to put on a bathing suit and go to the ocean after school.

I attended the local public school my first and second years of school. There was a large playground with a plethora of swings, slides, seesaws, and monkey bars. The schoolyard in New York was a concrete space useful primarily as a place to line up to go into class. I do not remember what I learned or who my friends or teachers were. Jumping the surf at the beach, playing at the edge of the water, and collecting seashells are fond memories. Jack and I painted seashells with the idea that painted seashells was a more profitable business than selling lemonade. All the other entrepreneurs were selling lemonade we wanted to be different. We got a fruit crate from the supermarket, painted "Seashells, five cents" on the side of it and set up shop on the corner of our street. We told passersby that we had the best seashell to be had in all of Florida and that our seashells made the best ashtrays in all of Florida. In the three days we lasted in business, we earned two dollars and twenty cents, which was promptly put in the piggy bank and credited, toward our college education. Well, it was a start!

One winter, Alice's brother, Bill Farrell, lived with us in Daytona. He was out of work and down on his luck. I remember his vermilion hair and thick bushy vermilion mustache. Tortoise shell glasses rimmed his face. He may have been in that period of his life referred to today as "finding one's self." Dad's description tended more toward "useless parasite." In any event, when Dad discovered his presence in Daytona, another notch was carved in the belt of the impending separation.

If truth were told, the family gossip was that Bill was escaping from an unhappy marriage and two children he could not support. Out of work and without a trade, he drifted from one meager job to another. Bill was the youngest and the only brother among five sisters who competed to dote on him. He loved the ocean and the sun but his fair skin kept him wrapped in sunscreen and large brimmed hats. There was a golf course abutting the ocean. His passion was to be outdoors all day and play golf. It is a rich man's game so the closest he got to his dream was a month's employment as a caddy. After that, he spent most of his time on the front lawn playing with me, and Jack. He tried to teach us to putt but it was a useless endeavor. We were too young but it did give him the excuse to set up a putting green on the lawn.

I thought Bill was fun. He was there for Alice when she needed a babysitter or someone to go to the hospital with her when Jack was ill.

She got a part-time job in a nearby nursing home. Bill was there to take care of us when she worked.

Fourteen

I must call Leonard to let him know this trip may take longer than I figured. Sara is not doing well and there are so many things to attend to. I discovered I need this time away from him and away from New York to sort out my life, our life. We are drifting without any real sense of what we are doing or where we are headed. Seeing Sara has brought back much of my past. I was reliving and rediscovering my entire life. I continued my one sided talk with Sara. Talking to Sara I was discovering where I had come from and trying to decide where I was going.

When it was time to go to high school, I made what turned out to be a life altering decision. The nomad life was not for me. I wanted to live in one place and go to one high school for the next four years. It was about that time that Dad's Sister, Mary, married. She married

Fred, a widower with two sons. Their mother was dead and like me, the boys lived hither and yon, but mostly with their mother's sisters.

We became an instant family of five. I moved in and was assigned to sleep on the living room couch. The apartment, a small one-bedroom with a large alcove, was located in the Chelsea section of Manhattan. The boys slept on a pullout bed in the alcove. It was a five-story walk-up. We lived on the top floor in the back. If you looked out the window, you had a choice of underwear to observe. Someone's wash was always on one of the clothes lines strung between apartment buildings. It is amazing how much you can learn about your neighbors by studying their underwear. I was embarrassed looking at my winter underwear on the clothesline. My aunt made me wear pink long johns that came down to my calves, and long heavy cotton stockings that ended tied in a knot somewhere above my knees. Not a pretty sight. She was convinced that in later life I would have rheumatism if I let the cold of winter get into the marrow of my bones. Well, I do not have rheumatism but arthritis is a problem. It was not fancy living but it was at least a permanent home.

Aunt Mary was a fastidious housekeeper. Cleaning was her life. Put it down, she owned it. We could never had a Christmas tree. It made too much mess. In addition, it had to be lugged to the fifth floor and then down again making a mess both ways. The furniture in the living room was covered with slipcovers, which were covered with white sheets, which were covered with plastic. "Things are expensive and must last," she would say. Most days you squeaked when you sat on the couch. On a warm day, you squeaked *and* stuck to the couch. I do not remember the color or the pattern of the couch or the chairs. I do not remember seeing it. My guess would be green floral. She loved green and painted every room in shades of that color. If we complained about sitting on six levels of separation from the furniture, we were told that the layers could only be removed when company arrived. We never had company. The few close friend of my aunt and uncle who visited infrequently, were not considered company.

My aunt did not understand much about electricity. She bought an oversized refrigerator and had the men from Sears put it in the undersized kitchen. The kitchen was so small we sometimes ate in shifts, three at a time. With a bit of luck, one of us would come home late for dinner. The problem arose when the men from Sears after dragging the refrigerator up five flights of stairs, discovered that the electricity in the apartment was direct current and the refrigerator was wired for alternating current. The problem could be solved by a twenty-dollar investment in a switch of currents. My aunt lived there for more than twenty years without switching the electrical current. She was a stubborn woman who would not allow herself to be taken advantage of by a corrupt electric company. Like my father, she believed prices were certain to come down.

Twice a week all summer, for twenty odd years, the little Italian iceman climbed five flights of steps, with a block of ice over his shoulder, and put it in the window box outside the kitchen window. The refrigerator was used to store dishes and dry goods. You could find the peanut butter and cookies there whenever scrounging for a snack. In winter, the window box was used to store perishable food with the natural ice provided by the New York winter. Not much could be stored so daily trips to the A&P were an essential part of life. Much of my childhood was spent going to the store. We were always in need of milk or bread. When money was tight, which was most of the time, we visited the German delicatessen downstairs for bread, milk, cold cuts, and other needs. He allowed us, and most people in the neighborhood, a running tab that we tried to pay off at the next payday. "Run down to Herman's and get a quart of milk. Tell him to put it on the cuff," was my Aunt's direction to one of us. I never saw Herman write on his shirt cuff but he did have a notebook with the account for each family in the neighborhood. When we went to the butcher shop, we were told to get a pound of chop meat and a hunk of boloney for the dog. Very few people had a dog but everyone asked for a hunk of boloney. It was lunch for the next day.

Aunt Mary was a petite woman who on a good day weighed ninety pounds. She kept her hair-dyed platinum blond and her fingernails trimmed to perfection. She enjoyed bright nail polish colors. During her poorest days, she managed to find money for a weekly trip to the beauty salon. She had enormous nervous energy that expressed itself in bouts of excessive housework. She was high strung with little patience if things were not going well. We learned to clear the room when her high voltage energy was about to explode or was at least on simmer. As a cook, she followed in the rich tradition of the Irish kitchen, well done is not done enough. She was a good woman who worked hard and loved us all. Her home was my first experience with family.

Fred was a quiet man. He sat in the big chair with his feet up on the ottoman, smoked cigars, and listened to sportscasts on the radio. He was convinced nothing would ever come of television. He never owned a television set. In his view, no one would sit in front of a small black box for more than a few minutes before getting bored. With radio, he was free to close his eyes, listen, and eventually fall asleep. He got out of his chair only to eat, to go to bed, or to go to work. He and Mary worked nights for the Schubert Theatre Organization. He was a ticket taker and she was an usher. Fred's sister-in-law, Eleanor, was J. J. Schubert's secretary. When I reached the age of sixteen Aunt Eleanor got me a job as an usherette at the St. James theater. The Schubert's owned most of the legitimate theater houses in New York. If a show was booked into the Schubert Theatre on 44th Street or the St. James Theater on 46th Street, it was sure to be a hit. These were two of J. J.'s favorite houses and he hated to see them dark. It was through Eleanor that Fred and Mary were fully employed most of their lives. Though they earned a meager few dollars a week, at least they were able to survive without being on welfare. For the Irish, welfare was a dirty word. Food was cheap. Bread was ten cents a loaf and twenty cents for a family size loaf. There were two hundred ways to cook hamburger and fifty ways to cook pasta. We survived and didn't know how to be deprived. After all, they were working.

The up side of things is that I saw all the shows on Broadway. Each Saturday morning, a visit to Aunt Eleanor's office yielded a note to the doorman at a theater and I was in for the matinee.

There was usually a seat in the orchestra someplace or else I sat down front on the steps. In time I became an enormous fan of the theater and in my own mind, a first rate critic of plays, actors, and directors. I read the *New York Times* review for each new show on the morning after it opened. Brooks Atkinson, the *Times* reviewer, was my hero. At the opening night performance of *Carousel,* I was standing in the back of the orchestra because the performance was sold out. Richard Rogers came by, saw me there, and asked why I did not have a seat. I had to explain I was a relative of the doorman and not a paying customer. I fully expected to be thrown out. However, he was gracious enough to smile and let me stand there. For many months, I told, retold, and embellished the story of the night I met Richard Rogers at the opening of *Carousel.* As Andy Worhol said, everyone has fifteen minutes of fame. That was mine.

Peter, Fred's younger son was my partner most Saturdays. Peter was about my age. We were good pals and went to the same high school. We argued about plays and performances, quoted lines from favorite shows, lived, and breathed theater. I don't think either one of us ever wanted to be an actor, but we both yearned to write the great American drama.

159

Stephen, Fred's older son soon began to drift in and out of the family. He did not like high school and had been thrown out of his share of schools. He was in and out of what were then called reform schools. It was never clear what he did to deserve a judge sending him away. I suspect his major crime was not attending school. He and his stepmother never did see eye to eye. Sometime during his sixteenth year, he disappeared never to return to the family. The last we heard he was living in Arizona. There is even a story that he received a degree from the University of Arizona.

During these years, Fred was the father figure in my life. He was there each day to help me with homework as well as to listen to me rattle on about everyday crises in the life of a young woman. At night at dinner, he engaged Peter and me in a competition he called "skull practice." We were quizzed on current events. He expected that we read the newspaper each day and were able to discuss the important issues of the day. We had to be able to recite all the states in the union and their capitals. We were required to discuss the plays we saw and the books we read. There was a time I could recite his favorite poem, *Jabberwocky*, by Lewis Carroll. ""Twas brillig and the slithy toves did gyre and gimble in the wabe: All mimsy were the borogroves, And the mome raths outgrabe..." is all I can manage now.

160

We could name all the Justices of the Supreme Court as well as all the members of the President's Cabinet. We could tell you what was happening in any part of the globe. We fancied ourselves experts in everything and we were highly critical of those who disagreed with us. We were convinced, that given half a chance we could run the world and do a much better job of it. Oh the arrogance! I shutter to think how stupid we were.

Mary was very proud of Fred and told all her friends that he was a graduate of Xavier High School, the Jesuit run military school in Greenwich Village. It was rare for a man of his age and from a poorer family to have a high school education and it was especially rare to be the product of a Jesuit education.

Aunt Mary and my father both had to leave school after the seventh grade. When Mary was four and Dad was two, their father died of cerebral meningitis. He was twenty-six years old. Their mother was a young uneducated Irishwoman living in a city hostile to the Irish. Job descriptions carried in the newspapers usually had the tag line, "Irish need not apply." The Irish lived in ghettos such as Hell's Kitchen on the west side of Manhattan between 18th Street and 40th Street and worked as day laborers doing the dirty work of building New York City. They

161

suffered much the same discrimination and loathing as the Black man. They worked and fought for jobs alongside the Italian immigrants and the Blacks who flooded the city in the early part of the twentieth century. Perhaps the competition for jobs caused the friction between the groups. It always struck me as odd that the folks from the Isle of Saints and Scholars and the folks who produced Dante and Michelangelo and who shared a passion for Catholicism could distrust and despise each other as they did. My father's constant counsel to me was, "Never trust an Italian." As I look at the people who are and have been important in my life, I find there are a significant number of people of Italian descent.

It wasn't until the Irish discovered they had a talent for politics that their lives took a turn for the better. Their facility with the blarney turned many an election. Among the Irish, there is more truth than fiction to the saying, "Vote early and often." They learned that political patronage is a proud and ancient tradition. They learned, too, to take advantage of the benefits and security of public service in the uniformed city services and in teaching. By the 1930s, almost every policeman, fireman, and teacher in New York City was Irish. They protected and educated successive waves of immigrants. It is a route succeeding groups of immigrants have followed.

I have no indication how my grandmother, Catherine White Connors, supported herself and her two toddlers after her husband, John, died. I imagine she washed clothes or did housework for the fancy uptown ladies as most Irish women did. The Irish are closed mouthed about family matters. I am not quite sure if it is because families are feuding and, therefore, not on speaking terms or if it is the result of an over developed sense of privacy. With the Celtic penchant for gossip and a long legacy of story telling, I can only speculate that feuding is the reason.

The genealogy handed down to me by my father told nothing of his father and little of his mother. Dad knew that his mother was from a small hamlet in Ireland known as 'Callaghan's Mill, County Clare, and that she had a sister who was a teacher and who met an untimely death on the horns of a bull. Dad never spoke of any aunts, uncles, or cousins. I was left to believe that grandmother had no family. Not much of a family history to dig roots into.

The truth is, as I later learned, that Catherine, born September 18,1872, was the ninth of ten children of Catherine Moloney and John White of O'Callaghan's Mill, Ireland. At least three other than Catherine came to the United States. Her brother, Thomas, met her at the boat when she arrived around 1900. Michael seven years older than Catherine, lived in the United States for a period, then returned to Ireland married and had at least one daughter. Julia, the youngest of Catherine's siblings, was the maid of honor at Catherine's wedding to John Connors when they married in New York City around 1901.

When I was about twelve, I recall Dad and I visited the Griffin family. Dad said Richard Griffin was his cousin. We went there only once or twice for Sunday dinner and then I never saw them again. Richard owned a riding stable and he trained horses for the New York City Police Department. In restructuring the family history, it is likely that the Griffins are the children of Julia White, Catherine's sister. What happened to separate the families is a mystery. Somewhere out there I may have dozens and dozens of cousins. Is it possible that Catherine and Julia were feuding?

My great-grandfather, John White married Catherine Moloney at O'Callaghan's Mill, Ireland on February 22, 1852. On the marriage register of the church, John's address was given as Gortaroma in the Parish of Clonlea. Today it is known as the Parish of Kilkishen. Catherine's address was given as Iragh. The priest charged three pounds to perform the ceremony, a large sum of money in 1852. It suggests that the family was well off. For the Irish that could mean as little as that you own the pot you pee in. After six hundred years of British rule, the Irish had little left but their sense of humor. This they burgeoned into a legacy for their sons and daughters around the world. After their marriage, the Whites resided on the Moloney farm at Iragh, which today is known as O'Callaghan's Mill.

For years, Dad and I asked every Irishman we met if he had heard of the village of O'Callaghan's Mill. No one knew the place. It proved a fruitless quest until a visit to Ireland in 1983 located it about six kilometers from Shannon Airport. I shall never forget the exhilaration I felt as I walked through the streets and visited the old gristmill of that tiny hamlet. I experienced the presence of my grandmother, her siblings, and her family. I had a sense of coming home, a sense of family, a sense of belonging. I realized the importance of roots without which we are un-tethered in the universe, wandering about unattached. I marveled at the courage of my grandmother and the millions of others who left small hamlets all over Europe to make a journey to an unknown continent in search of a better life. They crossed the ocean as steerage passengers suffering the discomforts of seasickness, cold and cramped accommodations, many riding out the trip in the hold of a barely seaworthy ship. My grandmother, as so many others, never saw their families again. What she found in New York may have been barely better than life under British rule in Ireland but was hardly welcoming.

Catherine White Connors married Patrick Carroll a year or two after her husband John died. True to form, neither Dad nor Aunt Mary spoke much about Patrick except to say they both intensely disliked their stepfather. They adored their mother and were not happy with the way their mother was treated in this new marriage. He, too, was an Irish laborer struggling to make a living. For whatever else he might have been at least, he was a good enough man to take on a woman and her two small children. A young poor Irish widow with two children had to settle for what she could get in order to support herself and her children. There was no social Security or Aid to Dependent Children.

Only recently did I visit Calvary Cemetery in Queens to visit my grandfather, John Connors grave. I stopped at the cemetery office to get a map and the number of the plot in which he was interred. It was located in the old section of the cemetery not too far off busy Queens Boulevard. I searched fruitlessly but could not locate it. Eventually two workers saw my distress and came to help. They walked up and down rows of gravestones with me. Finally, they found an oversized site between two markers. "This is it. It is here," they reported. I stood staring at the grass. There was no evidence that his casket was below. There was no stone or marker, or any indication that I was looking at a grave of a man who lived and fathered two children, and left a young penniless widow to raise his offspring. He was a man who was a third generation American, the grandson of an Irishman who as a teenager, migrated from Ireland to make a better life for himself. There are few things sadder than to spend eternity in an unmarked grave. There was not as much as an "X" to mark the spot indicating a human being had once been here on this earth. There had been no money for even a small stone or a small cross.

Great works of literature, music, and art are produced so their creators may live on after they have left this world. Fathers prize their offspring as bearers of their name and a memorial to their lives. Most of us settle for a gravestone as an emblem that we once existed. I cried for the grandfather I had not known and for my father who had little or no memory of him.

Dad told stories of being a workingman from the age of six. At that time, he sold newspapers to help his mother financially. By the time he was twelve, it was the point for him to

167

think of a career. They could not afford college, so a trade that would provide a good living was sought. Catherine had a friend who was in the roofing business. Dad was sent up to the roof to work with this man and learn the trade.

The sky over New York City was littered with pigeons. Every tenement rooftop housed at least one pigeon coop. Raising, flying, and breeding pigeons was an inexpensive hobby most workingmen could afford. A few yards of wire and a few boards put you in the pigeon arena. Before and after work, workmen would take to the roof and tend their pigeons. The allure of these birds was too much for Dad. He was soon an expert on birds and a total failure at roofing. He built a coop on the roof and soon had a flock of trained and loved pigeons. His career on the tar lasted about two weeks before it was declared over.

His next venture was to apprentice to Harry Lechner's printing business. This was more productive. He learned to be a linotype operator and remained at the same firm during his entire working career. Because he was such a fast operator, his workday was less than six hours in the late afternoon to mid-evening. He never did the nine to five routine. He enjoyed the mixed blessing of having most days free to spend as he pleased. He was out of step with the rest of the

168

world who were going to work five mornings a week and going home to dinner with the family each evening. Dad was accustomed to rising about nine o'clock, then going to the corner coffee shop for breakfast and to read the three New York City morning newspapers. New Yorkers never met a newspaper they could pass without reading. It is an obsession. There is arrogance in this, which leads them to believe they know everything about everything happening in the universe. It prepares them, as they will tell you, to have the solution to most world problems.

He developed a cadre of cronies, the retired, and the unemployed, who hung out in the local coffee emporiums. These Runyonesque types talked baseball, politics, and the fifteen reasons why the United States should give up sending money to support every foreign nation in the world. They were strong isolationists. They were also serious horseplayers. Not a day went by, which did not see a horse in the fifth at Aqueduct or Belmont that was the ticket to riches and the good life. Dad was a social gambler as he was a social drinker. His drinking was not excessive but only to be one of the boys. A two-dollar bet was the usual but, for a *really* hot tip, he might risk five dollars. As they say, you win some, you lose some, but only the bookie gets rich. At times, his involvement as a client of the bookies led him to try his hand at first being a runner, collecting bets for the bookie and, for a short time, as a bookie himself. He had too much time on his hands and needed a hobby.

Before off track betting was legalized in New York, every candy store, every coffee shop, and every small family grocery store had a resident bookie. New Yorkers bet on everything. Racehorses and the numbers were the most popular. Most people read the *New York News* and the *New York Mirror* newspapers as well as the *Daily Racing Form,* all of which carried extensive information about racehorses. You were told the lineage of each horse, performance in recent outings, and what his chances were on a dry or muddy track. You knew more about the horse than you did about your mother-in-law. Each gambler had a *foolproof system* for picking a winner. Use it and you can't lose! No one had enough money to bet on the stock market but most people could muster two dollars for a bet and have as much fun.

The fortunes of a bookie change from day to day. If it is a good week, you buy a black Cadillac, hire a driver, and take your friends to New Jersey to dine at the best Italian restaurant outside of Italy. I never figured out why this restaurant is always in New Jersey, but it is. It is not always the same restaurant in New Jersey. Every bookie knows a different one. However, it

170

is always the best outside Italy. Next week you sell the Cadillac and eat at the diner. At least this was Dad's experience.

Dad's aspirations to live life as a bookie were only slightly more successful than his endeavors as a roofer. The *big time* pigeons in the industry chased him off their turf. During his good days as a bookie, I frequently suggested that he buy a house so we could have a home. A good week produced enough money to purchase a small house on Long Island for ten or twelve thousand dollars. He was convinced that it was a lunatic idea to pay such an outlandish price for a house. He was convinced that prices would come down in a year or two. They never did. We never had a house.

Fifteen

City kids grow up playing in the street or in the empty lot on the corner of their block. You learn to be resourceful and creative when looking for toys. A ball, a broomstick bat, a rope, a few marbles, and a doll or two, carried you through childhood. A pair of skates and a sled made Christmas. You played outside and in between cars until dark then home, dinner, and homework. In the summer, you turned on the fire hydrants and scooted in and out of the cold water. My father talked about swimming off the docks on the Hudson River and hopping a free ride on the back of a trolley or bus to get uptown.

The pink spaldeen ball was the major treasure of every Manhattan kid. Everyone carried one in his pocket. With it, you were always prepared for a game of some kind as soon as one or two other kids came out of an apartment house and wanted to play. Usually the number of players determines the game. If there were two players, the first choice game was stoopball.

Most apartment houses had two, three, or more steps up to the entrance of the building. This is the stoop. The player, who is *up* stands at the stoop, throws the spaldeen so it hits the corner of the step and bounces off the stoop and high into the street. The other player stands in the street and tries to catch the ball before it bounces. If the ball is caught before the ball bounces, the other person is up. If not, the first player remains *up* until the ball is caught without a bounce.

Box ball was our version of tennis. The sidewalks in Manhattan are divided into square blocks of cement. Most sidewalks are two cement blocks wide. This game can be played with two, three or four players. Each player is assigned a box. The ball is sent to another box. It must not touch a seam of the cement. The player in that box must hit the ball to another box without the ball hitting a seam of cement. Only one bounce is allowed. If a player misses, the other player gets a point. Twenty-one points wins. A long wall against an apartment house or warehouse became a handball court. This, too, was played with the glorious spaldeen. I could not imagine Hilary playing on the streets of New York as I did.

The big game, however, was stickball. An adaptation of baseball played in the street by the boys and with the spaldeen and a long narrow broomstick instead of a baseball bat. The rules were similar to baseball except there were small differences to suit the requirements of a particular city street. The prevailing rules were the rules of the block on which the game was played. Any number of players was allowed as long as there was an equal number on each side. One sewer down from home plate was a single, two sewers was a double. Sometimes cars were used as bases. Two cars down from home plate was a single. Cross the street to the second car for a double or triple. Each street had its own team. Streets played each other for money. Rivalry was fierce and often involved skirmishes. There were no umpires or referees, which made for some interesting discussions. Bragging rights and girls belonged to the victors.

It was easy to tell the change of season. When everyone showed up wearing roller skates, you knew it was spring. It just happened. There was no plan or prearrangement. It was like the swallows coming back from Capistrano. Street hockey and the races were on. It was summer when marbles appeared. Winter was also the time for cookouts. We built fires in large metal trashcans and roasted potatoes. Only kerosene stoves burning in the kitchen heated many apartment houses. This meant only one room was warm. It often was warmer outside. Standing around a street fire eating roasted *mickies*, as we call the potatoes, was an Irishman's dream.

Hopscotch, jump rope and "*A*" *my name is Anna;* "*B*" *my name is Barbara...* were the games which occupied the girls. Hop scotch and "*A*" *my name is ...* were played with the treasured spaldeen ball and, of course, rope was used for simple jump rope and for double dutch. The queen of the game was the owner of the spaldeen or the rope. I once considered naming my first-born child, Spaldeen. The cement sidewalk was the necessary environment for all our games. While a tree grew in Brooklyn, there were not many trees and little grass growing in the Chelsea section of Manhattan.

Leonard's experience was so different. We were really two different people. There were few spaldeens in his life. The ball of choice in Scarsdale was the tennis ball played with at the "club" and in the traditional "whites." He went to Groton before enrolling at New York University. No wonder he married Whitney instead of me. Why am I always the outsider, the second best? I am still getting life's hand-me-downs. When I have a little more time I am going to have a good "feel sorry for me" day.

175

Parents never got involved in what happened on the street. There was no adult organization or supervision. We were on our own to work things out. It wasn't cool to let your parents know what was going on in the street. We learned independence and we learned how to take care of ourselves.

"Get out of the house and blow the stink off yourself," was a favorite expression of Aunt Mary. Not very elegant, but it was an effective way to tell Peter and me to go do something on a Saturday or Sunday afternoon. Since there was no money attached to her request, we went to the storage bin in the basement of our apartment house, dragged out our homemade bicycles, and went exploring. Uncle Fred had convinced us to accept the challenge of building a one of a kind bicycle built from odd pieces rescued from discarded parts left in back alleys or empty lots around town. I had a bike that was purple, blue, and yellow. The front wheel was slightly larger than the back wheel allowing the front of the bike to ride higher. As the bike gathered speed and rampaged downhill, I had a false sense of security and suffered less terror in the face of approaching traffic.

New York City was a wonderful place to experience the world in microcosm. Every few blocks put you in another ethnic neighborhood.

You heard a different language, unfamiliar odors greeted you, and you saw people of varying shades of color. If we rode uptown to 86th Street, we listened to German spoken and saw wurst hanging in the window of the butcher shop. On the street corner, vendors sold wonderful large salty pretzels. In winter, unmistakable aroma of roasting chestnuts lingered on every street corner.

The Armenians were on the eastside in the thirties, the Italians were in Little Italy near Greenwich Village. The Irish dominated the Westside of Manhattan, the Chinese clustered in lower Manhattan near the Bowery. The first generation of each of these peoples spoke their native language, and recreated their native customs and culture in the New World. Their children went to school, learned English, and assimilated. The third generation made their way into the professional class of the city and moved to the suburbs. As a child, I did not realize how fortunate I was to live in a culturally diverse city where I encountered every spoken language, every religion, every race, and every group in the universe. It was a second hand trip around the world; the only one a poor kid could afford. In many respects it was better than a trip around the world because I had the advantage of spending many years with a diversity of peoples, rather than a day here and a day there as a tourist. There was never the, "If it is Tuesday, I must be in 'Belgium'" syndrome.

If Peter and I were not venturing into neighborhoods by bicycle and did not have the price of a movie, we rode the subway through four boroughs of the city. A favorite Sunday outing was the subway to LaGuardia Airport in Queens to watch the planes take off and land. Nothing gives you wanderlust like an airport. I dreamed of some day saving the fifty dollars it cost to fly to Philadelphia and back for the day. It was the cheapest flight I couldn't afford. For ten cents, you got a ride to Long Island and the chance to walk around the airport all day. Air travelers were the most elegant folks around. They were very rich and very important. They didn't wear pink long johns. Some Sundays, Peter and I took a cruise. For ten cents, you could cruise all day on the ferry between the Battery in lower Manhattan and Staten Island. Or, for a change of scenery, you could take the 42nd Street Ferry and cross the Hudson River into a foreign land, New Jersey. From the ferry slip, it was an hour's hike up River Road to the top of the Palisades to Weehawken and the most fantastic view of the Manhattan skyline. We played in the park and on the statue of lexander Hamilton there. The statue marked the place where Aaron Burr killed Hamilton in a duel. Dueling was outlawed in New York so the two crossed the

178

river. It seems Hamilton made some derogatory remarks about Burr during the 1804 race for governor of New York. Burr didn't like it so he challenged Hamilton to a duel. Politics were rough in those days.

For us the city was the most alive in Greenwich Village, or *Garret City* as we called it, because so many artists were holed up in rat and roach infested warehouse lofts writing, painting, or composing music. We lumbered through Thomas Wolf's *Look Homeward Angel* trying to relate his struggle to come of age with our own. We were fellow artists, or so we imagined. Wandering through the Village, we looked at every hairy, gaunt, unkempt, passerby with a copy of Kahlil Gibran's *The Prophet* under his arm, as a future William Faulkner or Tennessee Williams. I think we thought that brushing elbows would make us artists, too. Could it be guilt by association? We sure hoped so.

Aunt Mary, a very practical woman, had little respect for what she considered the shiftless riff-raff in the Village. So when she asked Peter and me where we went, the answer was, "Out." "And what did you do?" "Nothing." The adventures we had were our secret. We prided ourselves with being *in the know* about every back street and mew in the Village as well as every street and neighborhood in Manhattan. New

Yorkers are accused of being the most ethnocentric people in the world. We flouted that tradition.

In her own way, Aunt Mary was a flamboyant woman. Because she worked as an usherette in the legitimate theater, I think she thought she was in show business. She talked about actors in a familial way as though they were her friends and family. She had strong likes and dislikes of them as people as well as professionals. As she often went back stage on a mission, she saw them when they were not *on*. Helen Hayes was a gracious lady and superb actress. Katherine Cornell was a bitch. I have it on good authority. She would not hesitate to instruct you in the Broadway stars who were authentic actors and those who slept with the producer to get where they got.

The excitement of a first night opening of a Broadway show thrilled her. The limousines rolled into 46th Street by the hundreds and unpacked their cargo of elegant theatergoers. This was in the days before blue jeans. New York City policemen, mounted on horseback, kept the crowds and autograph seekers from crushing the stars when they arrived at the theater. Broadway stars and Hollywood legends glittered into the house oozing glamour and style. Aunt Mary listened to their chatter and came home with first-hand stories. "Clark Gable was there. Clark told Carole..." She was a Broadway maven with the inside track.

Since she was in show business, she dressed and did makeup to suit the part. She went gray in her twenties, but I knew her only as a highly coiffured platinum blond. Max Factor and Helena Rubenstein were her patron saints. She was a tiny woman, less than five feet tall and under a hundred pounds. She loved spiked heels and suave black dresses. As one of the first women of her generation to work outside the home, she was more a woman of the nineties than one of the fifties.

Aunt Mary was a great fan of radio. She followed the fortunes and misfortunes of Stella Dallas, Backstage Wife, and Ma Perkins as though they were relatives. Peter and I, home for a Campbell tomato soup and peanut butter sandwich lunch, much preferred Lux Radio Theater. At night, we lived for Fibber McGee and Molly and Fred Allen. In my mind's eye, I could see McGee's closet and imagine all the things, which came tumbling out each time he opened the door. I never realized it was all done with sound effects and without a stage set. It was a further loss of innocence when I realized so much of life is smoke and mirrors. If you can't trust Ma Perkins, whom can you trust?

What little I knew about my birth mother I learned from Aunt Mary. My mother's death ruined Dad's life. They had been childhood sweet-hearts who married when he was twenty-one and she twenty. It was a brief marriage as I was born ten months later and she died from complications of toxemia four days after my birth. All remembered her as a pious and saintly woman mourned by my father and my aunt until the day each died. There were no accounts of anything she did. There were no tales of her childhood or teenage years. Her personage was a void.

Her holiness was affirmed in the most ambiguous terms. However, it was agreed by all that her sainthood was the result of her decision to chose my life in place of hers. The doctor advised my parents that he could save one of us, not both. Although the story was repeatedly relayed, so I would understand how important I was, it registered a different effect on me. The guilt clung to me like a wet leaf to tree bark after a rainstorm.

Dad never spoke about her but became sad when Aunt Mary mentioned her name. Consequently, Maura was spoken of only in Dad's absence. My maternal grandmother, Maura Kinsella Roberts was only referred to as *That*

Witch who treated her daughter poorly and perhaps abusively. What she did to her daughter was never cited. After my mother's death, all ties with her were broken. I never met her. I am very curious about her and my maternal grandfather. I think she was born in County Wexford Ireland but I know not where or when or how either of them came to the United States. I do not know if she or my grandfather had siblings or any other family either in the United States or elsewhere. There is some disagreement in the family as to grandfather's real name and lineage. Some think his name was Henry William Roberts, others hold out for William Henry Roberts. There is an apocryphal story that he was a chief of the Iroquois Indian tribe of New York State. When the Iroquois of New York go into the casino gambling business in this state, I shall pursue the matter of my being part Indian. Until then, yet another gap remains in my roots and identity.

The Irish people are garrulous by nature but inarticulate when it comes to handing down tales and folklore about the family. I believe there are two reasons for this. The *Feud* is probably the prime reason. If you get three Irishmen together, there is a good chance two of them are not speaking to each other. A feud can pass from generation to generation and long beyond anyone's memory of its origin. Offenses rising out of funerals, weddings and *the drink* are legendary. Relatives invited or not invited to a wedding may never speak to each other again. If an Irishman *owes a coach* and the debt is not paid at the next funeral, he becomes an outcast. To owe a coach means, we attended your family wake, were at the church for the Mass, and followed the funeral procession to the cemetery. We expect the same from you. Owing a coach is a sacred obligation. For the Irish, dying is an even more important event than being born. When you die, you go to your eternal reward. When you are born you, begin a lifetime filled with pain, struggle, and stress. The Irish never got over the English experience. In their minds, Irishmen are destined to be poor and persecuted. The Church also teaches that death is superior to birth. The Church celebrates the birth of its saints into heaven, not the day they were born on earth.

For whatever reasons, my father did not talk about anyone in the family other than his mother. Either Irish feuding or Irish shame brought on by a family member was the cause. I do not know. Every family had its drunk or a brother in jail as well as the holy priest or nun who prayed for the rest. For many years, I felt it was my fault Dad's life was in shambles. Had I not been born, he and Maura, his only true love, would have lived happily ever after.

Dad often came by to Aunt Mary's house on a Sunday afternoon so we could spend some time together. Sometimes we went to the movies. Radio City Music Hall was a favorite. There usually was a first-run movie and a stage show featuring the famous Rockettes. Sometimes we went to the Polo Grounds to watch the New York Giants Baseball team play. Dad was an avid Giant baseball fan. He never forgave them for moving out of New York. He hated the Brooklyn Dodgers with a passion that bordered on neurosis but, then again, that was almost normal among New York baseball fans. We rooted, hollered, and sometimes exchanged expletives with nearby Dodger fans. Sometimes we went to the Bronx Zoo or to the zoo in Central Park. Besides visiting the monkey house, the seals, and the polar bears, we walked over to the carousel at the other end of Central Park for a ride, or down to the lake and rented a boat for a row around the park. Dad was fun to be with and we always had a great time.

Sixteen

I t was on one of our Sundays together that Dad took me to Bickford's for lunch. This was a cafeteria one step up from the Automat but I thought it was La Cirque. I think I was in my first semester in high school. We sat down at a table and were soon joined by a man I had never seen before. He kept grinning at me and nodding his head in what I took to be approval. I had the feeling I was either being interviewed for a position or about to be sold into servitude. Eventually Dad said, "I would like you to meet your Uncle Bill."

My first reaction was to question where people were finding so many lost relatives. My second reaction was to tell Dad how surprised I was that he had a brother. It never occurred to me that Uncle Bill was my mother's brother! He and Dad started to talk about me as though I were not there. Bill commented on how much I looked like his dear sister Maura. He inquired about my school grades. He seemed genuinely happy to meet me. I found it reassuring that I looked like someone. For many years, I thought I was adopted and no one was sharing that with me. I looked like my father, but there were pieces missing. As I studied my new uncle, I found it unnerving to see him in possession of some of the same mannerisms I had. We had a similar smile and our eyes matched. I scrutinized him in an effort to get some idea of what my mother might have been like. He was soft spoken and gentle. His heavy New York accent was undeniable. I was fascinated. It seemed he lived in Chelsea all his life but we never came upon each other. We walked the same streets and visited the same stores. We went to the same movie houses. Perhaps we passed on the street without a clue to the other's identity. This could not have happened in Stokes Pines. New York is a city of anonymity, a place to hide, a place to be alone.

I cannot fathom why he showed up in my life at that point but he did. After my mother died, Dad disengaged all conversation between himself and the Roberts family. I never saw my maternal grandmother or my only uncle. No one, not even Uncle Bill, ever explained what happened. He often spoke of his sister but never of his mother. Oh, the Irish *curse* of burying the family instead of the *feud!*

187

Bill worked as a stevedore on the docks of the Hudson River waterfront. He was slight of build and never weighed more than one hundred thirty pounds. I wondered how he survived in a world where men tipped off at two hundred and fifty pounds and brawled over jobs and valued physical dominance above all else. Stevedores were, in a sense, day workers. No one was hired on a permanent basis. Any man who wanted to work showed up in the morning about seven o'clock for the *Shape*. They gathered around the headman who usually was the strongest, toughest man among them. If he pointed to you, you worked that day. If not, you took yourself to the local bar to spend the day. You did not want to go home to tell the wife and kids there would be no paycheck for the day. The opportunities for graft and payoff were rampant. My little guy uncle must have suffered many beatings on days he was chosen in favor of someone else. He also must have paid his share of kickbacks. Every week some colleague worked less than a full week, yet needed money for his family. Bill was known as a soft touch. He could be counted on to lend a hand. Was he a soft touch or did he fear being roughed up? He learned to ingratiate himself to the big fellows by becoming a runner for the bookies. In turn, the bookies protected him.

The following Sunday, I was introduced to my new Aunt Kitty, Uncle Bill's wife. She was a colorful, salt of the earth, old time original New Yorker, who grew up in a prominent German family in the Ridgewood section of New York who disowned her because of her unorthodox ways. She left home at about the age of fifteen and made her way in the world by singing in saloons and speakeasies during the prohibition years of the Great Depression. She had a throaty cigarette and whiskey voice and a heart of gold. She told stories of the gangsters and high rollers she knew and for whom she sang. You heard the same story perhaps ten or twenty times. Each time it was different, so it was hard to garner the truth. One story related her experience as saloonkeeper and madam in Philadelphia. The same story related to a different audience made no mention of Madam Kitty. She shared these stories only when we were alone. When my father or other members of the family were present, she made a Herculean effort to project a persona of *Miss Polly Perfect*. Dad did not like Kitty or Bill and thus I wondered why he introduced them to me. Perhaps Bill pushed the issue because he wanted to know his sister's child.

Aunt Kitty had a wonderful ear for language. Although unschooled, her life spent living among the many ethnic groups in New York allowed her to absorb their cultures and

189

languages. I heard her speak Chinese in Chinatown with the Chinese. She rattled on in the Puerto Rican dialect with her neighbors. She bargained in Yiddish for goods in a Delancey Street fabric store. She knew some German because it was spoken at home. She spoke Italian while shopping in the Italian butcher store as she ordered her meats and Italian sausages. Her French was sweet to the ear. I studied French in high school so was able to understand much of what she said. However, my French had a flawless New York accent while hers was spoken like my teacher's.

Aunt Kitty had an enormous love of people of all kinds. She found a joy in the diversity of the life and the people around her. I never heard her express a desire for English to be spoken, but she showed a great courtesy to all her neighbors by a willingness to learn their language and speak it as best she could. She lived her life among immigrants and the poor of the city. She was poor, but her soul was rich with laughter and merriment that so often hides the pain and hardship of the lowly of the earth. She adored Uncle Bill even though my father and almost the entire rest of the world thought of him as quite useless. Today she would be thought of as an enable-er for she babied him by tolerating his excessive intake of beer. She was mommy and he her little boy. They were both children but they

190

were loveable. Perhaps his life on the docks was tolerable because he was loved and babied at home.

For most of their lives, they lived in the basement of a run-down brownstone house on the Westside of Manhattan. It is a New York anomaly that we lived within several blocks of each other and had never met. Bill became disabled while still a relatively young man. He had complications resulting from his time of service in the army during the Second World War, and his strenuous life on the docks. During the war, he piloted a landing craft, which ferried soldiers from a naval ship to the beach at Guadalcanal. His nerves were decimated. He had met and admired Lieutenant John F. Kennedy, commander of PT Boat 107. His apartment was awash in Kennedy memorabilia. If he talked about the war at all, it was to praise Jack Kennedy, regular guy.

The last years of their lives were spent in a city housing project on 125th Street in Harlem. Both were disabled and living on Social Security. I helped them move into a one-bedroom apartment on the twenty-second floor in Building A of a sixteen building high-rise complex. Kitty and I went shopping with the allowance for furniture she received from the City, and bought three rooms of furniture. It was an instant home, all in one package, which included a complete

191

bedroom, living room, and kitchen. We put up curtains, bought, and hung a few pictures and plants. Kitty loved birds. As a house-warming gift, I bought her a canary. We packed their belongings and they left 30th Street to begin their new life.

The projects were home to the minority poor of New York City. At that time, they were peopled by a black population which had moved up from the rural south and a Puerto Rican population which migrated to New York with the intention of working to make enough money to return to the tropical delights of the Caribbean and live in relative splendor. Why would anyone choose to live in cold hostile New York when there are Caribbean Islands? The first generation did not give much thought to assimilation to life in a northern state. They did not learn the language nor participate in the life of the city other than to work, send money back to the family they left behind, and plan for their eventual move back to a better life in Puerto Rico. They were good people, but had little interest in caring for a building they did not view as their home. It was public housing and substandard at that. The hallways were covered with graffiti. Elevators were often out of order. It sometimes took a week to get a repairman there to fix things. To my unaccustomed Irish nose, the odor of garlic was overpowering. The walls rattled with the pounding of salsa music swelling in sheets of sound on every floor. There was an intensity of life and chaos.

It did not take long for Kitty to know everyone, every man woman, and child, in the complex. She became the honored and revered *Miss Kitty* who spoke to them in their native language and dialect. She told them off-color jokes in their own tongue and sat on a bench outside the apartment house drinking beer with them on warm summer evenings. She played with their children and told them wild stories of her childhood. If there was a Pied Piper in Harlem, she was it. The neighborhood was among the more dangerous in the city. The *Bodegas* were constantly subject to petty thieves. Gunshots rang out at all hours of the day and night. However, everyone knew Miss Kitty and her Bill. The community loved and protected them.

Each time I visited, there was another piece of furniture missing and something similar but older and in disrepair, in its place. One day it was a lamp; another day it was a chair, a bed, a table, and finally a couch. The replacements were older, shabbier and nothing matched. I asked but was never given an answer. In fact, there were several different answers but none made any sense. I was never sure if they needed money and sold off the pieces and replaced them from the

193

Salvation Army shop on Second Avenue or had given them away to people they thought needed it more than they did. There was always someone in the building in need of an extra couch or chair for a relative arriving from Puerto Rico. Kitty inherited from her family, one hundred twenty five graves at Cypress Hills Cemetery in Queens. As people in the building died, Kitty donated a gravesite to a family who might not have enough money to buy one.

When Bill contracted terminal cancer, we managed to get him into St. Rose's Cancer Hospital in the Bronx. The good Carmelite Sisters cared for him and eased the pain of his last hours. They comforted his soul and gave support and consolation to my devastated aunt. Except for me, they were alone in the world. I was Bill's only living relative. They never had children. Kitty's alienation from her family, which began in her early youth, continued throughout her life. Although she had brothers and sisters, she did not know where they were or how their lives fared. Perhaps they, like my Uncle Bill, lived just around the corner and were never aware of the presence of the other. I wanted Kitty to come live with us but she decided to stay among her project friends and family. It was a decision I did not understand until many years later.

Bill's funeral was my doing. Kitty was too distraught to think about it. I decided to have the funeral in my neighborhood. I did not realize it at the time but this was a huge mistake. I was unthinking and insensitive.

I called the undertaker, and asked him to arrange to have Uncle Bill's body transferred to his funeral parlor. I went with Kitty to her apartment to get the things needed. Bill would need a burial suit, shirt, tie, and his Army discharge papers. Since he was a veteran, he was to be buried in the National Cemetery at Pinelawn. My task was to find the discharge papers while Kitty collected the clothes. There was no special place to keep important papers, such as insurance policies, or discharge papers, or other family documents. Actually, neither of them carried any insurance. If they needed medical attention, they waited for hours in the emergency room of the nearest city hospital. They never owned a car. There were no bankbooks or checking accounts. They eked out their meager expenses from the disability check and the social security check that arrived each month. Many months food for the last week was purchased *on the cuff,* the credit bureau for the poor, from the bodega on One Hundred Twenty Fifth Street. Most people in the neighborhood bought their groceries at the bodega rather than at the A&P

because the credit system was better even if the prices were higher.

I emptied every drawer, cabinet, closet, and, shoe box in the apartment in a futile effort to find the discharge papers. A collection of shoeboxes divulged a collection of old coins, earrings, hairpins, 1965 World's Fair memorabilia, old movie tickets, and a lifetime collection of other treasures. Meanwhile as Kitty continued to pack a suitcase with several changes of underwear, handkerchiefs and a dozen pairs of socks she was sure Bill would need while he was away, I continued to unpack these articles and put them back in the drawer. She would retrieve them and put them back in the suitcase. As we did this, she chattered absent mindedly about how cold it would be in Pinelawn and how he always suffered with cold feet. I repeatedly asked where she thought I might find the papers we needed. The packing distracted her and I never got an answer. After I exhausted every possible hiding place, I stood in utter frustration surveying the living room. It was then that my eye caught sight of the papers, framed and hanging on the wall next to the picture of Lieutenant John F. Kennedy on his PT boat.

Kitty insisted on a two-day wake. We sat for two afternoons and two evenings. No one came. The people of the projects would not go to an unfamiliar neighborhood. Many worked during the day and did not venture out in the evening. We had a wake and nobody came. I am beginning to understand that my family is not good at wakes, funerals, or gravesites. If it were not for the United States Government, Bill, like my grandfather would be in an unmarked grave. The morning of the funeral, Kitty and I followed the hearse to the church for the Mass. My parish church is the size of a minor cathedral. From the back of the church to the altar is at least a city block in length. The pallbearers rested the casket at the back of the church and waited for the priest to greet us. He came with two altar servers and the holy water. Seeing only Kitty and me, he waited, thinking the rest of the family was on the way. When he realized the full complement of mourners was there, he seemed touched and a little embarrassed. I think I saw a tear in his eye. The church was empty except for two or three stray women saying the rosary. It was a long walk down that aisle to the front pew.

When we got to Pinelawn, I saw that the Army had prepared a military interment. There was a tent over the grave sight and fifty or so fold- up chairs were set out. Soldiers in full dress uniform were standing at attention. It was a non-descript gray windy day. Around us, several other soldiers were being buried. Some had large retinues of mourners. I helped Kitty out of the car and over to the gravesite. She was quite ill and moving slowly. The Army began without us. As soon as the casket was in place but before we were at the site, the honor guard soldiers fired a salute, folded the flag, and, as Kitty sat down, they placed the folded flag in her hands, recited their speech about a grateful nation and were gone to the next gravesite. It was over in a flash. We got back in the car, and drove home in tears and silence. It was the saddest funeral I ever attended.

Kitty lived several more years mourning Bill. She was quite ill and spent her time in emergency rooms and hospital wards. I once tried to move her from a facility in which I felt she was not getting good care to a facility with doctors whom I knew would give her the best. She refused to go. During her last days, we arranged for in-home nursing care. It was Christmas Eve and I was planning a trip to Canada. The nurses told me they did not see any immediate danger of death and suggested I go ahead with plans. At four o'clock, I got the call to come. Kitty was dying. I raced to Harlem. She expired fifteen minutes before I got there.

I called the undertaker. Kitty was lying in bed in the bedroom in the back of the apartment. As it was Christmas Eve, there was only one coroner on duty. We had to wait until close to midnight before he arrived, examined her and signed a death certificate. Meanwhile the undertaker and I sat in the kitchen drinking coffee and swapping funeral stories.

A curious thing happened. The doorbell rang and I was faced with a weeping Hispanic woman and her husband. Word had spread through the building that Miss Kitty had died. They were there to pay their respects. I directed them to the bedroom. For the next three hours, the doorbell rang. A steady stream of distressed friends and neighbors paraded through the apartment to say good-bye to Miss Kitty in the back room. I was deeply touched by their love for her. They would miss her, her smiling face, her generous spirit, her warmth, and her jokes. Some had furniture in their apartments that she had given them. One lady had a bed she needed for her two growing boys, another a couch on which her mother slept when she visited from Puerto Rico. No one should be embarrassed or feel poor in front of family. Miss Kitty did what she could.

The undertaker and I looked at each other and realized we were holding a wake in the apartment. They viewed the shaman of death in the raw without the mercies of cosmetics or the scent of lilies: without the parlor lighting to

199

suggest she is only sleeping. It is a parable the poor understand well. They live it.

After we were squared away with the coroner, the undertaker and his assistant put Aunt Kitty in the funeral van and the four of us drove home. On the way, Joe, the undertaker, suggested that I go on vacation and we would bury Kitty next to Uncle Bill sometime after Christmas. Until then, he would keep her body in the funeral home. Kitty was not a Catholic and, as far I knew, was not affiliated with any Church. Since we had the wake, there was little else to do but bury her.

About ten days into what was meant to be a two-week vacation, I decided I needed to go back to New York to take care of Kitty. I flew into Kennedy Airport and called Joe when I got to my house. He was at my door in fifteen minutes. I hopped into the cab of the hearse next to him and we took the Long Island Expressway to Pinelawn. This time no military honor guard met us. It was a bitter cold day in January. Temperature was probably down to five degrees. There was a cold wind blowing across the graves. I was reminded of Kitty's concern for Bill's cold feet. Mine were freezing. Joe and I were the only two people there as the workers placed the casket on the green coverlets of the grave. They finished their work and left us. Joe pulled out a prayer book and started to recite the prayers usually said by a priest. I answered for the congregation. I looked over and saw tears rolling down his face. I had to agree with him when he said this was the saddest funeral he had attended.

During the next few days, I went back to Kitty's apartment. For some reason when we left, I left the door unlocked. I let myself in and found all of the furniture gone, as well as the other household furnishing and the clothes. What were left were the picture of John F. Kennedy and a few of Kitty and Bill's personal things. There was precious little for me to dispose of. My initial reaction was anger. Then I realized Kitty would want it this way. Her things, such as they were, went to the people she loved and lived among. Either they needed them or they wanted a remembrance of Miss Kitty. I locked the door and returned the keys to the building manager.

Seventeen

In Pre-Vatican days, there were two kinds of Catholic, those going to church and the sacraments and those going to hell. We were among the latter. We had all been baptized, made our First Communion and Confirmation and dragged ourselves to church on Christmas and Easter. In terms of our relationship to the Church, we were *Match-em, Hatch- em and Dispatch-em Catholics*. We married in church, we baptized our children in church, and we went to our eternal rest with a church funeral. Everything in-between was not church business.

Aunt Mary was married to a Huguenot Protestant and Dad was not divorced but separated. Since both states were scandalous, we dared not show our faces in church and we dared not go to the sacraments. In addition, everyone was working very hard all week and needed Sunday mornings for rest and relaxation. In the

jargon of the day, we were *lapsed Catholics.* Unlike
other faiths, once a Catholic always a Catholic,
even though you renounce the Church and join
another group. So, you are not an X-Catholic but
one who is *lapsed.* My dictionary defines *lapsed* as
has been. I have always been uneasy with myself as
a *has been.* The Church never gives up hope that
you will come to your senses. I was in public
school, but Peter attended the parish school.
Aunt Mary felt that boys needed the strong
discipline and teaching of the Christian Brothers.
When I looked at the school holidays that Peter
enjoyed as opposed to those I counted on, I
found he was far ahead. Not only did he have all
the City, State, and Federal holidays to which I
was entitled, he also had a host of Church holy
days to enjoy while I was grinding away in school.
Life was unfair. It was, therefore, for the most
ignoble of reasons that I asked to attend a
Catholic high school.

It was a small co-ed high school on the
Eastside of Manhattan. The uniform for girls was
a navy blue wool A-line dress with a white Peter
Pan collar and cuffs. I was unaccustomed to
looking like everyone else, however, there was a
certain pride in the identity it gave me. In one
respect, it was a relief not to worry about clothes
every morning. In another, I felt ill at ease
wearing *Sunday Best* all the time.

The sisters, who taught us, moved in a mystical aura of blue habit and long black veil. Yards and yards of fabric hid all but their faces and hands. We stood when one of them entered or left a room. We greeted them with "Good morning, Sister "or "...afternoon," or, " ...evening, Sister." We prayed with them at the beginning and end of each class. We asked a heaven full of saints to help us do good, avoid evil, and get good grades. Our own prayers were more along the lines of requests for a date or a cure for zits. We prayed for the conversion of Russia from its atheistic ways, and we filled little cardboard cartons with coins to help the starving pagan babies around the world. It was from the holy practices and good intentions of the sisters that I was introduced to the liturgy and theology of the Catholic Church as it was practiced just prior to Vatican II.

It was in high school that I learned that if you go to Mass and Holy Communion on each of nine consecutive first Fridays of the month, you would go to heaven when you die. For many years, I tried to do nine first Fridays but, somewhere between seven and nine, my commitment broke down. Something got in the way each time. It was a missed first Friday in July or August, vacation time, or a Friday happened on a school holiday, that was sending me to hell. Eating the smallest morsel of meat on Friday could also get you on the road to hell. Modesty and chastity were *biggies*. Impure thoughts enjoyed even privately were a sure sign that you were on the road to depravity. A friend recently told me the story of an elderly man who remembered Sister Mary Passionella shaking a finger at him to admonish, "Young man do not entertain impure thoughts." "Today," he said, "impure thoughts are entertaining me."

My Aunt Mary was a Bible literalist. She interpreted the Garden of Eden story explaining that Adam and Eve's sin was fornication, or adultery, or something impure. I did not understand how eating an apple resulted in all the mayhem that followed. I got it into my head that the apple was a killer forbidden fruit. If you ate it, you were surely a serious sinner. For years, I would not go near an apple and wondered about folks who did. I did, however, love bananas.

There were big discussions in class about Darwin and his theories of how the world began. Father McCarthy insisted God did it in the six days described in Genesis and that Darwin was only fooling around with theorizing and was probably wrong. Father couldn't accept a monkey in his lineage. I, on the other hand, ambiguous about my own immediate ancestors, thought Darwin was on to something.

Saturday confession was the big event of the week. It was a "must" to receive the Sacrament of Penance at least once a week, or it was not safe to go to Holy Communion on Sunday. The presumption was that you committed at least one mortal sin in the course of a week. We are all sinners and mortal sinners at that. If you showed up at Mass on Sunday and did not go to Communion, the supposition from your peers was that there had been a wild night in the back of a Chevy. Sex was on all our minds. There was no lack of rampaging hormones. The trick was to stay alive until you could get to Confession next Saturday, or it was the eternal fires for you. One of my favorite Confession stories from the nineteen fifties was told to me by my friend, Carol. It is representative of how we all viewed the sacrament. Saturday afternoon came and Carol, as she always did, went to church for the four o'clock Confessions. Of course, she confessed the standard five impure thoughts, three lies, six uncharitable acts, and one disobedience to her parents. She felt pure again.

At six-thirty that evening, her friend Julia called and asked her to come with her to the seven o'clock Penance service. Carol explained she had already made her confession for the week. Julia was insistent and added that they would go for a coke afterwards. As she sat in church waiting for her friend, Carol mused on what the sisters and priests told her about the abundance of graces which come through the Sacrament of Penance. She pondered how wonderful it would be to store up more sanctifying grace. Moved by the Holy Spirit and having no sin to confess, she fabricated a sin and entered the confessional. "Bless me, Father, for I have sinned. My last confession was three hours ago. I kissed a boy one time...."

The priest on the other side of the screen in the confessional was the aging pastor. In many ways, he was a kindly man but had no tolerance for sins of the flesh. He was quite hard of hearing and did not realize how loud he spoke. His rage was heard throughout the silent church. Penitents in all sections discovered that Carol allowed her body to be used and abused by all sorts of lustful men. When she exited the confessional with ten *Hail Mary's* to say, she felt all eyes staring and thought she saw a few women with scarves over their heads discussing her shame. Those were days of innocence when we trusted everything we were told. The Church was our mother and every word spoken by a priest or sister was accepted as absolute truth. We were children, and the theology taught us was intended to convey Catholicism in a manner, which children could understand. So many of the good nuns and priests were not well educated nor were they rooted in solid Church theology. Often they substituted their own private piety for Church theology. The tragedy is that many of us never matured in the theology. The religion of childhood did not make the transition to an adulthood belief and practice. For many, their theological education ended with grade school or high school and with childhood.

Although the theology was not great, the sisters taught much that was valuable in making us responsible citizens. To be a good citizen it was necessary to be a moral person. This meant being a good Catholic. They taught us compassion for the suffering, as well as forgiveness to those who wronged us. They taught us generosity in our relationships and in everything we did. The everyday message of their lives was that of self-sacrifice and service to God and country. Not every sister was a model to be imitated but there were enough wonderful spiritual women to inspire us. We dreamed of going off to the wilds of Africa or the continent of Asia to be missionaries to save the souls of millions and millions of people living in the darkness of their paganism. Not everyone wanted to leave the United States, but we all were imbued with the desire to be of service and to sacrifice our lives for a great cause. Some of us became priests and nuns, some became politicians, and many went into the uniformed services to serve as policemen, firemen, and some got over it. I desperately needed a place to belong. I saw the Church as a permanent entity. I could depend on it to always be there. After all, it had been around for two thousand years. It was a family. I could belong.

By the end of my sophomore year in high school, my father was insisting that I leave school and go to work. He thought that educating a girl was useless, for within a few years, she would get married and never work again. Education for girls was a waste of time and money. Had I been a boy, he would have insisted that I learn a trade as he did. He firmly believed that a woman's work was tending to the happiness and comfort of the man. We were definitely of different generations on this matter. I was thoroughly enjoying high school and was not about to give it up. It was the first time in my life I had friends. I belonged. I was a member of a class, a school, and a religion. I had found a home and was very comfortable. My Aunt Mary was on my side, so in the end, I prevailed.

It has always been difficult for me to understand youth who clamor to drop out of high school. We struggled to stay in school at a time our parents could have used the extra income. Our parents thought a year or two of high school was enough education for any one. Everyone worked after school and summers. We delivered groceries, waited tables, cleaned fish in the local fish markets of the neighborhood, cashiered in small mom and pop stores all over Manhattan, and did any odd job we could find.

My first summer job was at Woolworth's Five and Ten Cent Department Store in Greenwich Village. I was hired as a demonstrator. At sixteen, I thought this was the career job to end all career jobs. It had a title, and there was something of *show business* about it. The product I demonstrated was a cleaning cloth that did not hold even the dirtiest of dirt from the grimiest of grimy surfaces. The demonstration area was on a counter at the front of the store on Sixth Avenue. When I was not engaged in demonstrating, I entertained myself watching the always-exciting happenings in the Village. It was in the days before the famed Village Halloween Day parade but then every day was Halloween. Cartoon characters roamed throughout the store handling then replacing trinkets before deciding to make them part of their fashion statement of the day. They fluttered and preened in the milieu of a hundred tittering shoppers.

A five-gallon glass bowl of water and the cleaning cloth were my only props. As shoppers passed by, I tried to fascinate them with this amazing product. First I immersed the miracle cloth in water, then bent down and washed a

210

section of Woolworth's heavily traveled floor. I showed my audience the now mired cloth then immersed it in the bowl of water. Miracle of miracles! All muck, dirt, and grime dissolved into the water. The miracle cloth was new again! The sales pitch I developed to accompany the demonstration was my first venture into public speaking. I loved it. I loved entertaining the Woolworth customers. I loved meeting people. However, the job lasted only one month. I was fired, they said, because I kept calling the miracle cloth a *rag* and because I was not the world's greatest salesperson. My weekly sales report was dismal. To a New Yorker, *rag* is a perfectly acceptable term for their fancy product. Their displeasure was a mystery to me.

The store manager at Woolworth's was a short round balding man of about fifty. The top button of his trousers was always open. The "v" opening at the top got larger as the zipper crept down to an open position. His stomach protruded over and hung down over his pants. His shirt buttons strained to remain closed. The spaces between buttons revealed flabby flesh and black chest hair. He had a wide space between his teeth and one gold cuspid tooth which made his grin that much more sinister. He spent much of his day at my demonstration site. His pornographic language and his leer made me very uncomfortable. I noticed the other salesgirls

211

ridiculed his behavior and told him to go fuck himself. I was frightened and dreaded seeing him each day. The tension between being nice to my boss and staying away from his unwelcome presence became increasingly stressful. It was my first encounter with what today would be recognized as sexual harassment in the workplace. I had no idea how to handle the situation, nor did I speak about it to anyone. I strongly believed that I had done something wrong. I felt ashamed. Being fired was a gift.

The next summer, I had a job as a clerk at a horse racing newspaper. It was on the third floor of an old broken down warehouse on 28th Street just a block from the Hudson River. I worked in the statistics department. It was our job to track the information about every racehorse in the country for each outing. I knew the age of every horse; what position he ran in every race of his career; how much he paid; the kind of track -- muddy or dry on which he did his best; who owned him; and which jockeys were his riders. Every horseplayer has a keen interest in the performance record and lineage of each horse. This material is updated and published each day and must be available to the touting crowd well before gate time.

I do not remember how I got this job, but I suspect one of the bookies in the family put in a good word for me. Perhaps they thought it my early training for the family business. Anyone who knows me can tell you, I have a pathological aversion to numbers. When presented with a set of numbers, my mind freezes. Numbness overtakes me so that I cannot function. My stomach churns and I get nauseous. I was desperate enough to long for a job in a fish market like normal people. I survived the summer but just barely.

Eighteen

There were only forty-five students in my high school class. We were a very close-knit group. We took the same classes with the exception that some took four years of French and others took four years of Italian. I was a Francophile as were most of the other Irish American students. I approached the language with disbelief that people really spoke that way. Neither could I believe that the Dutch wore those cute little wooden shoes or the Germans wore *leder-hosen* with funny little suspenders. As sophisticated as I thought I was, I was ethnocentric enough to believe that the entire world was just like New York or like Stokes

Pines. My French pronunciation was more eastside of Manhattan than Left Bank. *La Plume de Moi Tant* is about all that survived four years of intense language study.

As classmates, we did everything together as a group. Where you saw one, you would see all. There was a jukebox in the school basement lunchroom. Tables were never set up for lunch. We needed the room for a dance floor. We stood at the back of the long room to gobble down a peanut butter sandwich before we danced away the lunch hour. You never wanted to miss a day at school because you would miss too much fun. Going to class was a small price to pay for all the merriment. We developed good friendships and several marriages.

By the time I became a high school senior, I was looking at a nearly perfect attendance record as were several of my friends. We decided it would be a crime to graduate from high school without ever playing hooky. It was our custom to gather each morning before school at the corner coffee shop for coffee and a danish. It was there that we planned the mischief for the day. It was a lovely spring morning. Graduation was nearing and we were still virgins on the hooky circuit. Frank Sinatra was at the Paramount Theater on 42nd Street. Everyone swooned and passed out in the aisles. Despite the fun at school,

215

we longed for the experience of indulging our emotions and hopefully passing out in the presence of our dream man. Instead of walking down the block to school, my two best friends and I got on the uptown bus and headed for 42nd Street. As the first performance was at ten o'clock, we had two hours to kill. We walked around Broadway trying to be inconspicuous. We browsed in and out of the Broadway shops and took seriously the "Going Out of Business" signs in every store on the Avenue, not sophisticated enough to know that those signs were permanent fixtures on Broadway. They were intended to make the tourist believe a bargain was to be had. Broadway bargains were as good as a two-dollar bet on a three-legged horse. We had our fortunes told in the upstairs salon of Madam Bularga, an Hungarian Gypsy. We were all going to marry handsome millionaires, ride in limousines, and live in mansions on Long Island. At sixteen you need to believe in this. Guilt is a hydra-headed monster! It was everywhere. We were convinced that all eyes were on us and that a truant officer or policeman lurked behind each set of scrutinizing eyes. How could we bear the shame of being arrested and hauled back to school? What was worse, how could we face the wrath of Sister Principal? Worse than that, were we committing mortal sin? But the sinner, intent on the pleasure to be had in the sin, plows on into

216

inequity and, like Scarlett O'Hara, will deal with the consequences tomorrow.

The show was sublime. It was the first and last time I saw Sinatra in concert. He sang all the songs we listened to endlessly and several we had not heard before. We swooned in the aisles and along with several hundred other girls, tried to mob him on stage. We tried to hide out in the ladies room so we could be there for the one o'clock show. Security was tight; we were discovered and dispatched to the stage door alley. It was only noon. What to do? We couldn't go to school and we surely could not go home. We spent a miserable afternoon avoiding the law, missing the good time at school and wondering if we would be expelled from high school.

The next morning we were summoned to the office of Sister Principal. Somehow, she thought it strange that three young women who never missed class and who appeared to be in the best of health all got sick on the same day. We were in deep trouble because of playing hooky, so we decided to come clean and not lie about it. That would only make matters worse. Our confessions and deep assertions of remorse led Sister to take pity on us. We escaped with a lecture on responsibility, the value of our education, and the many evils that befall young girls roaming the streets. Secretly, I think she thought it was comical.

As close as we all were, no one talked much about his or her family. We did not visit each other's homes nor speak on the phone. In my case, it was because we did not have a phone. Aunt Mary thought it too expensive. Prices will come down.However, the basic reason we did not talk about family was that each of us had scandalous family secrets to hide. Divorce was forbidden but was everywhere. It was many, many years later that I learned that the parents of my good friend were divorced and her father remarried and was living three blocks away from his first family. She was terribly ashamed and embarrassed by this. She lived in fear each day that this secret would be discovered.

The father of another friend left his family to live with another woman in common law and father three children. They all attended the same school. My friend went to great lengths to disassociate herself from the second family by maintaining that the mutual name was a coincidence. She told people her father died of a heart attack many years before. I was in a similar situation. Dad insisted that our story to the world was that my mother died at childbirth, Dad was a widower, and I was an only child. It bothered me that we did not see nor speak of my beloved

218

brother and stepmother. I knew that they lived in Massachusetts but I did not know where. Each week, Dad sent his child support money for Jack to the court, which forwarded it to Alice. Of all the odious things in my father's life, paying weekly child support was the most galling. He constantly complained. It was such a pittance; I wondered how Jack and Alice could survive. I wondered where and how they were living. As a widower, Dad enjoyed the attentions of the wives of all his friends. He was invited to dinner and frequently an unattached woman was his dinner partner. Married women are obsessed with match making. A good-looking unattached male was fair game to be stalked and tied with the marriage knot. Many saw themselves as my stepmother. It wasn't until some woman began to talk about commitment and marriage, did Dad reveal his married status.

Beneath the surface of the carefree life we led in high school, there loomed a dark side. The fun and frivolous existence was a facade to hide the internal chaos consuming us. If you do not take life seriously, you cannot be hurt by it. So, we played and pretended all was right with the world. I was dangling somewhere between a child and an adult and not wishing to go in either direction. Childhood was painful. I belonged no place. I was everyone's couch guest. I had no roots or rituals to ground me or to give me a sense of security or a sense of person. There was no notion of family. I was going no place and had no place to go. I was always out of   step with the rest of the world. A child has little imagination for "what might be" but only for "what is." What is will always be. So, while I dreamed dreams and constructed scenarios of a life I wanted for myself, my ghetto mentality never really believed that life would ever be any different from the life I knew. I was the third generation to grow up in a lower middle class Manhattan neighborhood and had no hope of anything but a future of duplicating the previous generations. I was convinced my trivial life was set in stone.

Since life is meted out on a string, we never get more than a glimpse of it at a time. We don't recognize patterns or fully understand the relevance of even the minor decisions we make and how they are probably part of a gigantic schema of our miniscule corner of the universe. To know, in one big-bang epiphany, on the first day how our lives will unstring, would make our days dull indeed.

My decision to change from a public school to a Catholic school seemed germane only to a shameful desire to add vacation days to my school calendar. It proved to be a key life-changing resolve. A metamorphosis was waiting to happen. My senior year in high school was an absolute nightmare. Laughter and playing the clown was the armor I embraced to hide the sheer panic and anarchy churning inside. Playing the village idiot seemed a better route than letting the world know I could not handle things. However, the boat I thought I had all to myself was jam packed with my classmates. We were all frightened of the future and our place in it. Too bad we did not have enough sense to talk to each other about it. Graduation time was fast approaching, and I had no clue what to do next. I suffered from terminal senioritis! It was time to move on and I did not know to where I should move. Nothing in my life made sense and life had little or no meaning.

During four years of high school, my peers and I were instructed in the teachings of the Roman Catholic Church. We attended Mass and received the sacraments regularly. So far so good! However, when the subject got around to questions of birth control and abortion and, for some of us, me included, even the existence of God, there was many non-believers. We argued vehemently with the priest who taught Apologetics and the nuns who instructed us daily about faith and morals. So much of what was being taught did not square with our experience and of the reality we saw around us. We did not take God or religion very seriously. We especially did not want God or the Church to interfere in our lives. As young adults, we felt the need to discard all forms of authority -- whether parental or ecclesiastical -- and be free to live as we pleased. We could not define adulthood as being responsible to God, country, and family. Our concentration was on the new found freedom we enjoyed. We interpreted this freedom as the freedom to do anything we pleased.

I had a special problem with the existence of God. How could a just God allow evil in the world. What proof was there that God existed? We lived in a world that believed science was the only god. If a hypothesis could not be tested by scientific experiment, it was not valid. We were asked to accept the existence of God on faith. Once God and I agreed on each other's existence, I was faced with the implications inherent in this acknowledgment. At the same time, I was filled with awe of the new horizons opening up in my understanding of the world, its history, its science, and its literature. My twelve years of education were paying off for I finally began to love reading and studying. For eleven years, I was a ho-hum student given to cramming the night before an examination. I saw no value to anything I was being taught. Now I wanted to read everything and study everything. In addition, there was an intense desire to share my excitement with others. I wanted to make the wonders of the world come alive for others as it was becoming for me. It was then that I decided that I wanted to be a teacher.

It was about December when my brain started to synthesize the information that teachers and others had poured into it during the years I attended school. I began to see how things were connected to each other. I think my teachers taught in isolated units and no one connected them for me. Rain was rain and no rain was draught; deforestation was taking down trees; soil erosion was whisking away good topsoil, etc. This is perhaps a primitive example, but no one connected the dots for why and how things related to each other and were part of a continuum. I think my head was the product of my early education that, á la John Dewey, taught only particulars were truth and there were no universals. There is no universal truth, nor beauty, nor love. When you add up all the particulars of history or philosophy or art, you are left with a subjective view of life that has no meaning other than what an individual assigns to it. Nothing seemed related to anything. Nothing had much meaning. For me it was a "so what world."

I began to think about the big questions of life and death and what it all means. I was coming up with nothing. My life became less and less fun and increasingly filled with panic and pessimism. I started hanging out in the school library looking for something to read which would help me understand my world and myself. It was impossible to talk to my father or Aunt Mary. Their solution was, "Get a job and don't worry about it." That, of course, is what they did and their lives were working out just fine. I was looking for something more that just getting a job. I wanted meaning in my life. I wanted to get out of Chelsea and break the three-generation cycle in the same neighborhood. It was impossible to talk to my peers for, as the old saying goes, it was a case of the blind leading the blind. Further, who can admit to a peer that she is a confused, semi-adult without a clue to what she is doing?

One day in the library, I came across a copy of Thomas Aquinas' work. The question and answer format interested me. He raised and answered many of the questions whirling around in my head about the existence of God; what life means; and what is our purpose in this world. I am quite sure I did not understand much of what I read, but the writings did give me an anchor, a place to hang on to, and a frame of reference on which I could build meaning into my life. I was fascinated and, at the same time, embarrassed to have anyone know what I was reading. For my classmates, I would be the recipient of world class teasing. At home, I would be looked at as having gone off the far end of the pier. Therefore, my visits to the library were discrete. I think the librarian wondered about me and about my odd taste in reading. I was searching and had no clue where to look or for what I was looking.

All of this came pouring out as I sat in the darkened hospital room. I wanted Sara to know everything about me. I wanted her to know how important she was to me. For many years, I was angry about what life dealt me. I was angry about being tossed about from place to place. I thought of myself as homeless and without family. I was insecure about my place in the world. I grew up without a mother and with a part time father. It was time to grow up and decide who I was going to be. I could decide to spend the rest of my life wallowing in self-pity or I could decide to get over myself and build the life I wanted to have. I made a conscious decision to get over it and move on.

The education of my formative years ended. The child within me was dying. It was time to leave childhood and discover my kismet. The time was near. I was on the brink of making another one of those life-altering decisions. As I thought back on my life, I realized it might have been different from the experiences of many; but it was rich, full, fun, and filled with interesting and wonderful people. Now there was Leonard.

I learned to have a sense of humor about myself and about the absurdities of life. I learned not to take myself too seriously. I learned to appreciate and enjoy the persons who were in and out of my life. By some standards, these people might be considered a motley collection of role models, but they were good to me and loved me. Each one gave me something of themselves that enhanced my life. Perhaps my birth mother was not there but others including Sara, and my father were there who took her place and loved me. If loved we will survive. Because I was loved, I survived. I had to tell Sara all of this. Although she was not there for the years of my adolescence, she was always a part of my life. I had to tell her about it.

The first light of morning was graying outside. Sara was asleep but breathing heavily. The bustle of the hospital morning was heard in the banging of breakfast trays and the chatter of the day staff arriving. Leonard called to up-date me in on the events of yesterday. The contract for the commercial building we hoped to sell was signed. A closing date was set for May third. He was living in my apartment and being sure to water the flowers. He wants to know when I am coming home.

A sweet ache of missing him fills me. I am restless with longing for his body, for the wholeness his love brings to my spirit. I long to lay down with him and have his tongue linger in my mouth and on my breast. Now I know that I have loved him since our days in college when I dismissed his abandonment of me as the loss of just another school time crush. I resented Whitney for depriving me of Leonard for so many years. It did not occur to me to resent Leonard. I had forgotten about the choices he made. For the first time in my life I was truly happy. Leonard and I belong together and yet....

I was telling Sara everything. Why could I not tell her about Leonard? The door opened and Putty fluttered in in a fury of palpitations and bearing coffee and a donut for me from the hospital cafeteria. Putty was always out of breath and not the slow moving stereotypical southerner. Five children, a husband, home and farm to care for puts the lie to the myth. Harry arrived right behind her. I was taken back by his appearance. I did not expect him to look the same as he did when I was a child but I was not prepared for what I saw. The years had settled on him like rainwater in a neglected basement, musty and moldy. No longer the poster boy for sartorial excellence, his shirt and trousers had a polyester lived-in quality.

227

He had a small limp from a motorcycle accident he suffered in his late fifties. There was a slight tremble in his right hand. Putty later told me it was the result of a stroke. His eyes, though framed in wrinkles, still looked out on the world and found joy. We hugged. I asked about his family. Hortense died last year but Lena was still working and still taking care of him. The children were all married and living in different parts of the country. He had eleven grandchildren, at least at last count. As he said, his expectations for life were to just keep breathing.

The doctor came in and told us Sara would probably last this day but not many more. Her breathing was heavier and her sleep was deepening. We kept talking to her. Harry teased her about how stressed out she became because of his idiotic behavior. What did it matter now? He loved her. He would miss her. Besides Lena, there was no one in the world who would put up with him. He was an old, still penniless man sick from a lifetime of avoiding reality, a charming peter pan of seventy.

Putty suggested since I needed a break it might be a good idea for Harry and me to go to dinner. We had much catching up to do, besides, she made dinner for the children this morning, and all Ethan had to do was heat things. Harry knew a wonderful little out of the way restaurant,

228

which specialized in, pulled pork. We could talk and treat this northern gal to some good down home cooking.

As we walked out of the hospital, he headed for the Harley-Davidson leaned along side the building. It was good to be rid of the odors of illness and the pall of death, which hung like the silent tower clock ready to strike the day's final hour. I put on the helmet he handed me and we headed out to the freeway toward downtown Taylorsville. He still had the ability to scare me half to death with break-neck speed and a weave and bob through traffic. "Some things never change," I thought.

The pork pull restaurant turned out to be a country roadside nightspot. The parking lot was rapidly filling up with other motorcycles, pick-up trucks, and small, old model cars. As in most Southern towns, people seemed to know each other or at least greeted each other as friends in good old southern hospitality fashion. They were a circle of regulars who loved to two-step when not fishing in the creek or hunting quail. There was a shotgun rack and a box of shells in the cab of each pick-up truck. There were signs everywhere saying, "No alcoholic beverages allowed on the premises." People alighted from vehicles swigging the contents of a bottle enclosed in a brown paper bag. Harry pulled his cache from the saddlebag and offered me the first drink. He had moved up from the moonshine I remember from my childhood to Seagram's finest.

It was dinner hour and only later would the fiddlers with shit-kicking music tune up. We were able to find a small table far away from the bandstand. Harry was very direct. "How old are you now; must be near forty?"

"Thirty-two," I corrected.

"Pity, good-looking gal like you not married. Too much education, I reckon."

He clearly saw me as the dreaded *spinster* and therefore not quite a woman. He was convinced one of "'em little ole Stokes Pines boys would have married me and been happy to do it." I should have stayed in the South. His niece Hilary on the other hand married three times and had five children. She was living up north someplace, no one knew where. She was a strong-headed gal who listened to no one. She should have been spanked more and spoiled less. It was a shame about her and Sara. It was slowly killing Sara.

I filled him in on the years since we last met. It took six years but I finally worked my way through college. After that, I was too busy building a career to think about marriage. I didn't quite make it into teaching but had a fairly prosperous real estate business. New York was a Mecca for men all wanting a relationship and even some who looked for permanence in marriage. I was not ready. Perhaps I had seen too much that was wrong in marriage. Now, suddenly in mid-life, love had come. I told him about Leonard.

It was nearly eight o'clock. The band warmed up and two-step dancing brought everyone on to the dance floor. It wasn't long before Harry spotted his regular dance partner and excused himself. After all these years, his motor was still running in high gear. Uncomfortable with ogling from cowboy booted, jean-clad gentlemen on the town, I took a taxi back to the hospital. I would see Harry there in the morning.

A sobbing Putty met me in the lobby. Sara passed away about twenty minutes ago. I had not been there. I have heard that sometimes the people we love choose to pass on to the next life when loved ones are not there. It is an effort to spare pain to those who may not be able to deal with events. Putty and I stopped by the roadhouse to tell Harry then drove back to Stokes Pines in silence and sobs.

Nineteen

After Dad's funeral I went to the hall of records in Queens and asked them to search back twenty years to find the formal separation papers for Alice and Dad. I had to know where they were. I cannot imagine why I did not look for them years ago. The pain of living without them got buried as one year passed into the next. It takes a death to remind us of what is important in life. Then it is too late to heal the years.

I was able to get the last known address for the family. There was no telephone listing for that address. I decided to call the police department in South Boston and ask if they knew the family. They were aware of an Alice, John and Catherine. I was convinced I had the right family. Catherine had to be Jack's wife. The police would not give me the telephone number but promised to forward my telephone number to Jack. Alice was still alive. My heart was pounding. I had not seen Jack or Alice since Jack and I were children. I wondered if they hated me. I wondered what their lives were like. I was almost sorry I found them. I could not bear the thought of them hating me. I still loved them very much despite the many years of separation.

It was now ten o'clock at night and no telephone call from Alice or Jack. I contacted the police early this morning. Perhaps they forgot to notify Jack of my call. Perhaps he was not interested in speaking to me. I was about to lose the most cherished memory of my childhood, the days Jack, Alice and I spent together.

It was ten thirty when the telephone rang. The gentlest, kindest masculine voice said, "Hi Maura. It's Jack."

I could feel a small thunderbolt go off in my head. Those simple words, "Hi Maura. Its Jack," I had listened every day for the past twenty years to hear those words. Why had I not tried to find him years ago?

"I guess Dad died. I'll come to New York in the morning and give you a hand with things." Still the generous Jack I remembered. "Mom says hello."

Alice was alive. Did this make Dad a bigamist? How ironic, an entire life avoiding commitment to wife and family and in the end has two wives and two families. I told Jack the funeral was over and everything taken care of. I just wanted to let him know.

We talked for two hours. The years between us disappeared. It was as though we had never been separated. He was so easy to talk to. We laughed and got filled in on each other's lives. He was a physician. He and his wife Catherine had three young sons. Alice had been totally crippled for ten years. She lived with his family and played grandmother to the boys. Her influence on all of them was a great blessing.

I hung up the phone and cried, saddened by the loss of so many years without my family. We missed so much of each other and for what? I decided against tell Jack about Dad's other wife and family. At this point it served no purpose.

The following weekend I flew into Boston and took a cab to Jack's home. New doubts surfaced. Like a flat line on a screen closes the distance between two worlds, we were closing the years between us. I was frightened we would not successfully cross over to each other after so much time. A gray New England rain played on the windshield. The wiper blades like two metronomes kept time to the rhythm of doubt beating in my heart. Would Alice still think of me as her daughter?

"We're here lady. Are you going to get out or do you want me to let the meter run?" The driver's crisp Boston accent jarred me back from my loose-footed thoughts.

Medville is a bedroom community thirty miles from the center of Boston. It has all the amenities required by the upper middle class: good schools: some of the best recreation areas in the country: safe streets and a low crime rate. My brother the doctor was doing very well. Jack talked about going to medical school from the time he got over wanting to be a fireman. Growing up neither of us had any money for college much less medical school, I marveled at how he managed to do it. I was very proud of his tenacity in the face of the financial hardships he faced.

When Jack opened the door I was stunned at what I saw. He looked like, sounded like and gestured like Dad. He had the same

235

gentle soft voice and quiet manner. I speculated he must have a wonderful bedside manner. He probably could tell a patient he suffered from leprosy and make him feel good about it. His body shape, all front and no rear end were exactly like Dad. His was the same curly coal black hair. My thought was that while he lives Dad lives.

Like so many doctors, Jack had married a nurse he met when he was an intern. Catherine was a quiet woman who doted on Jack and the three boys and cared tirelessly for Alice. The three boys, about ages six, ten and twelve, looked on in bewilderment at this strange woman whom their father introduced as Aunt Maura. They had always thought their father was an only child and their grandfather died before they were born. Jack thought it easier to tell them that story than to confuse their young minds with the crazy details of the real saga. There would be time when they got older. I cried when I thought about how much dad missed by his alienation from Jack and Alice.

We went up stairs to the middle bedroom where Alice sat propped up in bed with pillows on all sides. She had no use of her body from the waist down. I leaned over and kissed her. We both fought tears. I looked around the room and saw the pictures of Jack and me that I remembered form our childhood. There too was the framed clipping and picture of dad that appeared in the New York News Enquiring Photographer so many years ago. It was quite yellow but showed Dad as the young handsome man I had almost forgotten.

She told me how much she loved and missed me all these years. Whenever she spoke to Dad, she asked to see me but he was not open to that. She showed me album upon album of pictures she had of Jack and me as children. Some I had never seen before. As she talked, I realized that even after so many years and so many bitter encounters, she was still in love with Dad. It was more than I could bear. My emotions were welling up like ocean waves. It was then I realized there are losses, which need not be except for our own stupidity.

It was a great weekend. We talked and talked and talked. Catherine too was filling in the blank spaces that Jack was reluctant to share. She got a better understanding of her husband. Alice scrubbed floors and held three jobs to raise the money to put Jack through medical school. During the summer of his third year in medical school Jack thought about leaving school and getting a job so his mother did not have to work so hard. Alice arranged for him to get a job in a meat packing plant for the summer. The thrill of blood soaked smelly clothing and the odor of slaughtered beef soon convinced him that medical school was a much better rout. He returned to school in the fall. Alice was a wise woman who knew better than to argue with her strong willed young son.

Jack and I became instant friends. We often comment that the best way to raise siblings is to have them raised in different parts of the country and by different people. That way they have a fighting chance of becoming friends. I bonded with Catherine and the boys. It was as though we had never been separated.

Twenty

SAra's funeral would be very different from Dad's or from Cousin Nanny Lee Clark's send off. It would be in a funeral home in Taylorsville, done by a real undertaker. There would not be cucumbers placed on her eyes. The sun was signing a sweet tempered day, a bright moment; another soul separated from its body and returned to the eternal cycle of the cosmos. We wait our turn piling up the toys and treasures we shall leave behind. It would be a pleasant day for folks to gather to say good-bye. I was anxious to greet old friends. I would strain to remember some faces now gnarled and wounded by time. Perhaps a voice would strike a note and I would remember. We make distances between each other without knowing when, or how or why. One brief day fades into another and a life is gone before any recognition of its presence.

Putty, Harry and I made the arrangements. We picked out a cherry wood casket and ordered three wreaths of flowers. Sara loved the tall red callas, which grow in the warm southern sun. Harry did a good job of getting the word out. By the evening of the first day of a two-day viewing, Sara's surviving siblings arrived along with a respectable number of the population of Stokes Pines. Roy was in California but expected to be here for the service. Millie and Jake, now married to each other, came in together. Jake, Putty's brother, two years younger than Millie was in love with her when we were children. He tormented her day after day; until she was so frustrated, she chased him up the elm tree in Sara's front yard. When I think of Jake, I see him sitting high up in the "vee" of the tree dodging the sneakers she continued to hurl at him and laughing a demonic young lad laugh. They were still farming tobacco on the fifteen acres his father gave them as a wedding present. To supplement their income, Jake took a job at the cotton mill in Taylorsville. Their three boys helped on the farm and went to school in Stokes Pines. We talked about our summers; swimming in the river, the birthday parties and how well Sara treated us.

There were many faces missing, the result of early deaths or serious illness, which kept them homebound. Daisy died several years ago but her daughters came. When I was a child, they looked so much older than I. Today we were almost contemporaries, separated in age by only ten years. There were new faces, faces I did not know but people who came later into Sara's life. We talked, cried, and remembered.

We drove in procession from Taylorsville to Stokes Pines to the small Methodist Church I remember so well. The roads were paved now and the red clay was confined to the road banks. New houses dotted the landscape. Stokes Pines was no longer the rural tobacco neighborhood I knew but had become a bedroom community for Taylorsville and the larger towns around. There were few farmers and fewer still raising tobacco. I saw the new brick post office and the new branch office of the Taylorsville Bank. The Stokes Pines Diner and the bank startled me most since neither existed when I last visited. Old tobacco barns, half roofed, vine draped, still stood in deep grass as ghostly reminders of another day. A few cows meandered away the sunlight hours in open fields. There were mailboxes on the side of the road at the end of each driveway. I was reminded of my daily trips from Sara's house to pick up the mail for there was no delivery service. Sometimes I walked, sometimes I rode Molly, and sometimes Harry took me on his motorcycle. I was aware of another purgatorial moment in my soul as I pined for the good old days.

There were workers in the field but they were not the Black people of my youth. Putty told me they were Mexican migrant workers who came up from Mexico each year to bring in the tobacco crop. They lived in old trailer camps off the main road and out of sight of the immigration officers. They sent money back to their families in Mexico and what was left they spent whooping it up on cheap whiskey on Saturday night. They bought ten year old American cars, which they drove back and forth from North Carolina to Mexico. They were good workers and other than a bit of drinking, they minded their own business and bothered no one. They stayed the season then moved on. The Black workers had long since left the farmlands and moved into the surrounding cities or moved to the industrial north where there were more jobs. Putty said that without the Mexican workers, it was impossible to bring in the crop. The old log and gas heated trailer units, which looked like cargo containers, replaced mud tobacco barns. The few mud barns I observed along the roadside were falling down and in need of serious repair. Most of the half moon outhouses were also gone.

Wallace was standing at the edge of the church cemetery still wearing his cover-alls and

242

his large brimmed straw hat. His heavy work shoes were covered with red clay mud. He was more stooped over than I remember yet his fingers were still tobacco gum yellow. A self-rolled unlit cigarette clung to his lower lip. He did not come to the funeral home instead he remained in Stokes Pines and honored Sara by digging her grave. He wanted to remember her as she was in life. He was silent and deeply moved at the loss of his best friend. He nodded to me but said nothing. I knew he was glad to see me and happy for Sara's sake that I had not forgotten her. We shared a moment of silent understanding and silent remembrance before I went into the Church.

The service was brief since the minister was newly arrived and did not know much about Sara. There were conflicting views about Sara from the various community wags he talked to while preparing his remarks for the service. He did not want to risk praising or damning her lest he alienate some element of the congregation. He did mange to say he heard wonderful stories of her especially from the younger members of the community. He took the opportunity to remind each of us that one day we would all appear before the alter of God to give an accounting of ourselves and that we should prepare for that day by mending our ways. The fires of hell and damnation were still raging in Stokes Pines. Each phrase of his spirited homily were punctuated by loud "Amens" and "Lord Jesus be praised" from the regular church going members of his congregation. I scanned faces and saw there were some who believed Sara was among the damned. I wanted to scream out at them but thought better of it. I knew they were wrong and besides, what difference did it make?

Wallace was one of the pallbearers who carried the coffin to the grave he readied for her in the church graveyard. Harry, Roy and four of the grandchildren were the others. As they lowered her casket, I saw that her head would be below and between Miss Lucy and Mr. Tom, who were finally reunited in death. Three graves over, there was a headstone marked, Edgar Deveaux. Putty explained to me that yet another of Mr. Tom's offspring surfaced in the last ten years. His wife demanded he be buried in the family plot in the church cemetery. After Sara was in her grave I briefly walked through the cemetery and read the names on the headstones. Twenty-five years of my relationship with Stokes Pines was laid out before me. I remembered a story for each headstone I saw and said a prayer for each.

We left the cemetery and went across the street to the parish house to a luncheon prepared by the women of the church, the polite keepers of the Sabbath who did not count Sara among their number. Sara's sisters surrounded and sat me down in a corner of the living room. They were most anxious to hear all about me and especially to hear about Dad. They were always very fond of my father and thought it the great tragedy of Sara's life that they never married. They reminded me of how much she loved him and of how much she loved me and wasn't it a shame about Hilary and "No," I did not know anything about Hilary. The north is a big place and not at all like the South where everyone knows everyone. I had to tell them that dad died a year ago to the day.

On the trip back to Putty's house, we drove by Sara's. The white picket fence was missing slats and those still standing were in need of a fresh coat of paint. High grass and weeds made it difficult to get to the front steps. I wanted to hook up Molly and mow it. We walked up the steps to within inches of the door and stopped. Neither of us had the will to go in for we feared the loss of a childhood that may never have been. Our child minds build idyllic dreams to live in when our realities become too painful.

I stayed on with Putty for another three days before returning to New York. We talked, cried, hugged, and talked about everybody and everything. We laughed, told, and retold the story of Harry and his two families living in the same house. Today it seemed less a calamity than it did years ago and more a funny quirk of a story. Today we were less concerned with the moral issues of the situation than with wondering how two women managed such an arrangement. Putty's children found all this difficult to believe. Leonard called everyday anxious to determine when I was coming home. There was business that needed my attention.

Putty and I swore to keep in touch on a regular basis. I drove back to Fayetteville, dropped off the car, and took the two o'clock plane back to New York.

Twenty-One

I bought the *New Yorker* before I got on the plane but was unable to concentrate on it. A grandmother fresh from visiting her daughter and new grandchild sat in the seat beside me and insisted on filling me on every detail of the birth and delivery. It was a long labor before one sympathetic intern decided a caesarian would be necessary. No, I do not have children and yes, I do know what I am missing. Yes, it is too bad.

I had to feign sleep before she paused in the monologue. I did not sleep for my mind was troubled by the events of the last few days. It was not Sara's death or seeing old friends that

247

bothered me but there was gravel grinding in my gut. There was no serenity to the nostalgia walking through my mind in sensible shoes. Instead, it ran as if in stiletto heels leaving deep hurtful imprints.

I could not get Leonard out of my mind. We talked before I took off. Things were settled. We could not wait to see each other. We missed each other. Leonard was leaving his wife and two children. We were to move in together. We were in love. Finally, love and permanence would be my life. Why was I fretting about this? Just when you think the world is safe, the small, unexpected things vandalize you; rearrange your cosmic scene. Thoughts about dad and Sara crowded in on me. The parallels between them and Leonard and me became stunningly clear. Was I to be the other woman? Are we destined to repeat the sins of the past? Does life come full circle in time? I was terrified.

My plane landed at LaGuardia on time. Leonard was there to meet me. I was hungry for the comfort and passion of his body. We went to our favorite little Italian restaurant on 9th Street. Carmine showed genuine delight in seeing us and showed us to the small table for two, which we had come to think of as our special place. He knew the red wine we enjoyed so did not bother to ask but brought it to the table.

Clams casino and shrimp marina were more to my taste than pulled pork and so I ate and drank with abandon. We were so anxious to talk that we fell over each other's words and had to repeat many things to be sure the other heard. Things were good at the office. We had two new clients; he and Whitney each had spoken to a lawyer; it looked as though it would be a messy divorce because Whitney was being unreasonable; she would not let him see the children; she wanted more money than he could afford. My stomach contracted into knots. We made love but it was not the same.

There was too much to do at the office to think about the dark skies gathering over a pond of alligators. We settled into a routine of work and lovemaking. The commissions from the two new clients Leonard secured while I was away, yielded commissions of nearly half a million dollars. We were in negotiations with the Trump people to represent them. We had caught the brass ring at Coney Island. Whitney called daily, and sometimes hourly, with one demand or another. However, now that there was more money available her tone softened to include her longing for him: the children's need for their father and the tragedy of disrupted lives. She wanted him back. I could see that he was torn. Had my own life taught me nothing? My life is like the short neck puffin's world, etched in crooked lines in sand where each cruising wave which climbs the shore: or fly by night wind cruising through, feels free to rearrange my cosmic scene, to shift existing symmetry. There are no stable landscapes.

There is a circle of time, which brings things around again. It wasn't until the day Leonard got off the phone, turned to me and said, "That was F W – first wife," that I realized where we were going. A dull blackness of silence built up between us. We both knew what was coming. That night we turned the key in the lock and walked out of the office. Leonard took the train to Westchester. I went home, made a cup of tea, and decided to get a cat. I'll call Jack in the morning and tell him I'll be up to see him, Catherine, and the kids on Friday evening. Thank God for baby brothers. They are family.

About Margaret C. Offenberger

Margaret C. Offenberger had a career as an English teacher, and school administrator. She was a reporter, columnist for a local community newspaper and founder of Northeast Career Institute, a business school for women returning to the workplace. Her poetry is published in *Readers/Writers Quarterly*, *Time of Singing*, and *Wellspring Journal*. She is the winner of the 2003 *WellSpring Journal* award for excellence in poetry. She has also written a novel for young adults which explores the pangs of first love among teens, called *My Igloo Is Melting* and a book for parents preparing to send their first child off to college called, *How To Survive Your Kid's College Education*. She holds a Master of Arts degree from the University of the City of New York, Brooklyn.